ONLY THE TRUTH

ONLY YOU, 2.5

ELLE THORPE

For anyone who has ever made a mistake, owned up to it, and asked for forgiveness. None of us are perfect.

xxx

1

———

BREE

The second hand on the wall clock ticked on silently, my impatience growing every time it moved. There was a special place in Hell for people who continually ran late. Nothing annoyed me more. Though, I didn't know why I'd expected her to be on time today. She hadn't been on time for any of my other appointments either. "Just go on through to her office, Miss Jacobson. She'll be right with you, Miss Jacobson," I muttered under my breath to the empty therapist's office. Yeah right.

I straightened my pencil skirt, smoothed over my work blouse, and sighed. It wasn't the poor receptionist's fault, and I was being catty. At least I recognised it this time. Closing my eyes, I counted backwards from one hundred, breathing deeply. By the time I got to single digits, the bubbling anger had diminished.

The door behind me finally opened, and a short, dark-haired woman strode into the room, unhurried despite the fact she was over thirty-five minutes late for our five p.m. appointment. She deposited a pile of papers on her desk before sitting primly in her over-sized chair. "Bree. It's been some time."

"Six months."

Dr Guzman scribbled something on a notepad. "So, fill me in." Her gaze tracked carefully over my features, and I straightened my spine, folding my hands neatly in my lap. "How have you been?"

I plastered a smile across my face. "Great. Really great, actually. I have my own apartment now. It's only small, but it's in a great area. I enrolled in a Naturopathy course—"

"Naturopathy? That's…interesting."

I forced myself not to roll my eyes. I still worked my day job, as a makeup artist on a local TV soap, but after the breakdown of my last relationship, I wanted a change. Makeup appealed to my creative side, but I needed something that would exercise other parts of my brain as well. The mentors who ran the course had warned us we'd be given grief for studying alternatives to Western Medicine. They hadn't been wrong. My own mother had scoffed when I'd told her about it during our annual phone call. She'd called it 'hippy rubbish' to be exact. But if I hadn't bothered getting into an argument with her, I certainly wasn't going to try to explain the benefits to this woman.

So, instead, I carried on as if she hadn't spoken. "I've also been doing yoga and meditation and I've taken up cycling. That bike seat is the most contact my vagina has had in that time, too."

Dr Guzman looked up sharply, her pen hovering in midair. "Excuse me?"

My face flushed hot. Oops. Too much information. "I'm still not having sex, is what I meant."

"Right. Right. That's good." She moved to her laptop and scrolled through a file before turning back to me. "You don't have long left on your celibacy vow. Only about a month, according to my records. You've kept it this whole time?"

"Yep."

It had been one of the easier aspects of my therapy. Doctor Guzman had pointed out on our first session that I'd bounced from one toxic relationship to another, ever since I was old enough to realise boys existed. She'd made me write and sign a contract, stating I would avoid relationships or casual sex for a year while I worked through my issues. Not that she could enforce it, of course, but she'd pointed out I needed to make things right within myself before I could take on someone else and their needs. And, at the time, I was so sick of men, it hadn't been difficult to swear them off for a year. Other aspects of my reinvention had been much harder.

"And the anger management course I suggested?"

"Yes," I reported, legitimately pleased to be able to answer in the affirmative. Unlike the last two appointments, where I'd had to answer no because I'd skipped out on going. "I completed it last week. It was great. I really think it's helping. I feel less... highly strung." That was mostly the truth. I did feel less highly strung...when people didn't keep me waiting for forty minutes, anyway.

She raised an eyebrow. "Hmmm..."

I held onto my fake smile, but irritation crept up on me. I hated when she did that. I was here, on time for my appointment. Unlike her. I was talking. Why did she have to *hmmm* me? The woman reminded me of my mother and the disapproval I'd put up with for my entire life. I didn't need this judgement. Not when I was paying her eighty dollars an hour to fix me. The silence drew out between us as she waited, and I studied my shellacked nails, pretending not to know what she was waiting for.

She gave in first. Ha. "And your sister?"

Ugh. There it was. The one thing I hadn't done and the one thing I really didn't want to talk about. "What about her?" We both knew I was stalling, but she played along.

"Did you speak to her, like we discussed last time?"

My fake smile faltered.

"Bree. Don't you think you need to speak to her?"

"No," I stated dully.

She frowned, her eyebrows pulling together in the exact same way my mother's used to.

I really needed a new therapist.

"Fine," I huffed out. "I'll call her." Maybe.

"Today?"

I winced at the thought of making that call. Of speaking to the sister who had been a surrogate mother to me when our own was too busy with her career to care for the children she had never wanted.

The same sister who had then run off and married my high school sweetheart.

We hadn't spoken in years.

I'd let the trauma fester to the point it affected every part of my life, creating a temper I couldn't control. I'd explode into a fiery outburst at the smallest upset. It had almost become my trademark. But after a year of therapy, painstakingly fixing myself, I'd come too far to not finish the process.

"Fine. Today."

***

IT WAS WELL after six when I finally got out of the therapist's office and unlocked my bike from the stand. Dr Guzman's offices sat amongst several other medical practices and a mixed martial arts gym, with a combined total of three off-road parking spaces. It was impossible to get a spot, so I always cycled.

Normally I enjoyed the ride, as it was only around fifteen minutes from my apartment, but as I pedalled along the side of the building, all I could think of was the late hour. How I should have driven because I had a huge exam tomorrow, and between Dr Guzman being late, and now having to ride home, my study time was slipping away. I'd be pulling an all-nighter at this—

"Fuck!" a deep voice yelled as something huge ploughed into

me at high speed. I careened off the path, wobbling wildly onto the road. Mother of God! What the—

I didn't even get a chance to do any yelling or swearing of my own before my tyre hit a pothole and I crashed headfirst into the unforgiving ground. My helmet cracked as it hit the road, my cheek scraping along the tar in the process. My head spun, but it was my bare shoulder and arm that took the brunt of the fall.

I slid to a stop, my legs tangled around my bike, my skin probably left behind me somewhere judging by the stinging pain in my arm. Damn summer evenings. If it had been winter, I might have had some protection from the road, in the form of a jacket or coat. But this thin blouse had no chance.

At least I was close to medical help, I supposed as I lay there. Though, I blinked at the sky, wondering how helpful a therapist, a dentist, and a gynaecologist would be with probable broken bones and a concussion. I almost laughed. It sounded like the beginning to one of those jokes. Three guys walked into a bar…

As I pondered peeling my aching body off the road, a face appeared above me. A ridiculously handsome face. Dark hair. Hazel eyes. Scruff covering a strong jaw. If I hadn't just been nearly killed, I might have tried slipping him my number.

Why was I even checking him out when I'd just been mowed down? Maybe I really did have a concussion.

"Shit, are you okay?" he asked.

I groaned, my body protesting my attempts at moving. "Something the size of the Titanic just hit me, and now I'm a bloodied mess in the middle of the road. Do I look okay?"

I finally managed to get myself to a sitting position. Frig, my arm really hurt. I glanced down at it and grimaced. Yep, there used to be skin there. "What the hell just happened?"

The guy bent down and lifted my bike off me before he squinted at my wound. "I kind of ran into you. I was coming around the corner, and my phone was ringing, and I was trying to find it in my bag. I didn't even see you. I'm so sorry. Here, let me help you up."

He extended a hand in my direction, but I just stared at it, my brain not comprehending what he was saying. He ran into me? With his car? I gazed past him. No, he'd been on a bike, too. I could see it abandoned on the ground over by where he'd run me off the path. But, he was on his phone? WTF?

I was banged up and now going to be even later for my study session after I went to the ER and got myself fixed up, all because he'd gotten distracted by a phone call? Who was on the other end? The Queen?

The simmering anger I'd been working so hard to keep in check for months now threatened to erupt. Breathe, Bree. Breathe.

But then I saw a badge, dangling from his pocket, *Dr Damien Farrow* printed in neat type beneath a photo of his smiling head. His *stupid*, smiling head! You had to be kidding me. My barely in check rage bubbled over. Fucking doctors!

"You could have killed me, you douche nozzle! Why didn't you just let it go to voicemail? Are you really so important you *had* to take the call that very second?" I went to rub my aching arm, but my fingers came away sticky with blood. My stomach rolled.

"Shit! This is going to need stitches!" My voice came out high and squeaky, and I was probably overreacting, because I had a tendency to do that, but damn it, today was not my day, and I'd had enough. People sucked.

I expected more apologies and maybe some grovelling for forgiveness, but Dr Dickhead's lips curved up and, to my astonishment, a chuckle rumbled out of him. "Feisty, aren't you?"

My mouth dropped open. Scratch that about overreacting. The guy probably had awards for asshattery.

"What?" he asked as he took my arm, being careful to keep his fingers away from the blood. "It's a graze. You'll be fine."

"Fine? Easy for you to say. It wasn't your head cracking off the ground! What kind of doctor are you anyway? Don't you have some sort of duty of care to help the people? I could have a concussion for all you know. You didn't even ask me how many fingers you're holding up or anything."

"True." His voice was irritatingly calm in comparison to my yelling. He took my jaw between his fingers, tilting my head. I stilled as his gaze met mine. There were flecks of gold in amongst the hazel, and they were surrounded by long, dark lashes. The skin at the corners crinkled as if he smiled a lot, and there was a twinkle—

A bright light nearly blinded me, causing my eyelids to slam closed. I swatted his hands and doctor's torch out of my face. "What are you doing?"

He threw up his hands in frustration. "Since you implied I was being a shit doctor, I'm checking you for a concussion. How many fingers am I holding up?"

"Oh, for frig sake." I scrambled to stand, pulling my bike up with me. My head felt intact, I was good to go. "I'm fine."

"Your shirt is ripped, and you're bleeding. At least come back to my office. I may just be a gynaecologist, and not much good with concussions, but I can at least fix up a graze for you."

I snorted back a laugh. "You're a gyno?"

He frowned. "I specialise is gynaecology and fertility. Why is that funny?"

"Because you're entirely too young and good-looking to have your head between any woman's legs, unless you're—"

He raised an eyebrow as I realised what I'd said. Shit! I definitely had a concussion. I needed to go to the hospital. "I'm going to go now."

"Have dinner with me tonight?"

I spun back to where he stood with his arms crossed over his chest, one eyebrow raised as if he'd laid down a challenge.

"Why on earth would I do that? You just ran me over with your bike."

He shrugged, an annoying half-smirk, half-grin spreading across his face. "You've got attitude. I like it. And you really may have a concussion so you shouldn't be alone. Plus, you think I'm handsome."

"And arrogant. And possibly blind, considering you didn't even see me riding right in front of you. And anyway. I don't date. So, no thanks. I'll pass." I pushed my bike away, walking it a few steps before I swung my leg over and found the pedals.

"Shame," Dr Knob-Jockey called from behind me. "Because for the record, I'm really good *every* time I have my head between a woman's legs. Not just when I'm at work."

2

BREE

"Move, Sass, you're wrecking my system," I complained to Sassenach, my furry, grey fluffball of a cat. I'd named her after a character in my favourite book, because she was a bit on the uppity side, just like Claire from *Outlander*. Sass ignored me and settled herself in the middle of the dining room table, right on top of the notes I was trying to work through. She eyed me with the same attitude Dr Jerk Face had accused me of having earlier.

Ugh. I did not have attitude. I just didn't put up with people's shit. There was a difference.

I'd decided to forgo the emergency room visit, concluding, on my ride home, that Dr Dumbass was right. My arm didn't need stitches. Instead, I came home, cleaned up, and shoved some food down my throat before settling in with my books.

Moving Sassenach off my notes for the third time, I used my free hand to pull up the website of the online university. But instead of the white, green, and blue logo that normally greeted me, I got the *there is no internet connection* error page.

Great. This had been happening more and more lately, and it was really beginning to grate on my nerves. I probably needed to

9

invest in a new router, or some other piece of Internet-related equipment, but with the astronomical amount of money I'd shelled out for this course and the necessary text books, I didn't have a spare cent to my name.

I clicked my Wi-Fi name when the list of available networks showed up, pointing a finger at Sass who was stealthily trying to get back on the table. It was already nine p.m. If I could study until midnight, or maybe one a.m., I'd get through all the notes I wanted to revise, and I'd be able to go into tomorrow morning's exam feeling confident. The homepage finally loaded, and with Sassenach pinned to my lap, I finally got to work.

For exactly seventeen minutes.

The door to my neighbour's apartment slammed, and a loud, masculine laugh echoed through the walls, startling me out of my herbal botany bubble. Something heavy was dumped on the floor with a thump. A female voice called something I couldn't make out, then someone cranked up a stereo.

The inhabitants cheered.

Nineties rock pounded through the wall.

You had to be kidding me.

They'd only moved in over the weekend, and they were having a party. On a Monday. Seriously? I pulled on some head-phones, but even a white noise app couldn't drown out the thumping bass, the constant slamming of doors, and multiple loud voices. Sassenach jumped off my lap and took refuge under my bed when they turned on a karaoke machine.

God-awful singing splintered through the thin plasterboard walls.

I cranked the white noise app as loud as it would go, recon-nected the Wi-Fi, which had dropped out again, then forced myself to concentrate. But it was impossible. Over and over, I read the same lines, and an hour later, I was still on my first page of notes.

"Ugh!" I huffed as I threw a pen at the wall. It bounced off and dropped to the floor harmlessly. Realising I didn't have another, I stomped across the room to retrieve it. This couldn't go on. I was going to have to do something or I'd fail my exam.

This was a good opportunity to use some of the strategies I'd learnt through therapy and the anger management course. I'd never really been able to deal with conflict in a proactive way; instead, I was always reactive, and the course had taught me that wasn't the best way of dealing with problems. I'd just go over there and calmly ask if they could keep it down. No need for dramatics or hysterics.

I cracked my front door open and stuck my head out to find a hallway full of people. Some carried boxes into the apartment next door, others just stood around drinking from beer bottles.

What was this, a frat house? I ventured a foot into the hallway, but no one paid me any attention, and I made it through the crowd to the neighbour's door.

Standing in the open doorway, I took in their apartment. Moving boxes were piled up, open drinks and packets of chips sitting precariously on top. Half a dozen people sprawled over two large lounges, all hooting and hollering at a man with two women draped all over him. I'd found the source of the woeful singing making my ears bleed. The noise probably drowned out people in the next building, but I knocked pointlessly on the doorway anyway, too uncomfortable to just waltz in and demand to speak to the new tenant.

The knock fell on deaf ears, no surprise there, but my movements must have caught the eye of the guy singing. He swung his head in my direction, his eyes locking with mine.

My mouth dropped open.

Recognition flickered in his eyes, and a grin spread across his face. "Hold my beer, ladies." He offloaded his microphone and drink to one of the women, who booed him for leaving, and sauntered over to me like he was Damon Salvatore from *The Vampire Diaries*. Good-looking, no doubt, but as arrogant and cocksure as he'd been a few hours earlier when he'd not only run me over but asked me out. The skin on the back of my neck prickled. This guy had some nerve.

"I thought you said you didn't want to go out. Now you're stalking me?"

Oh, for Christ's sake. "Unlikely. I'm just unlucky enough to live next door. I came to talk to the tenant."

He leant one hand on the wall beside my head. His t-shirt lifted revealing a slice of toned abs that was mouth-wateringly distracting. "You found him."

"You." I choked on the word, all thoughts of abs flying out the window. "You live here?"

"Just moved in yesterday. Looks like we're neighbours. Lucky me."

OMG. Could this day get any more ridiculous? "Lucky how?" Lucky I didn't punch him in the face perhaps.

"Because now I have the opportunity to ask you out again." He tilted his head to the side. "You won't turn me down twice. Next time I ask, you'll say yes."

I cocked an eyebrow. "You're awfully full of yourself, aren't you? In there, with women hanging off you, then over here begging me to fall at your feet."

He chuckled. "I was hardly begging, sweetheart. And you don't look like the sort of woman to fall at anyone's feet. I like that."

The guy was too smooth. Too charming. Too good-looking. Time to make an exit.

"Just keep it down. The walls are thin, and I've got stuff to do." He probably wouldn't, but I'd been the bigger person and asked politely.

He pushed back off the wall and gave me a mock salute. "Not a problem, neighbour." He strode across the living room and pulled the microphone plug from its socket, the speakers squawking in protest. He held it up, waggling it at me as his friends groaned and complained. Then he began herding them out the door.

Huh. Well, what do you know. I gave a tiny nod of thanks before retreating to my place.

I settled back in at my table, pleased with how that little exchange had gone, if not pleased about the new neighbour himself. I could handle an arrogant, party-throwing doctor. And I was proud of myself for dealing with the situation without it descending into a screaming match. There'd been too many of those in my past. Bree 2.0 was calm, cool, and collected. And she was here to stay.

Music still filtered through the walls, but it was at a much lower, more acceptable volume, and I recognised the notes of Bruno Mars' *Gorilla*. Slow, sexy music. Nothing like the pounding bass or the pop music karaoke tunes. I actually liked this song. And the slower tempo was easier to study to. My eyes were heavy, but if he kept it to this sort of music, I could get two hours of study in, grab a few hours of sleep, then get up early to make up for the time I'd missed. The study session could still be salvaged. I pulled my laptop closer. Then a loud moan echoed through the wall.

A woman's voice followed up with, "Yes!" and, in utter disbelief, I turned to stare at our adjoining wall. For the next two minutes and seventeen seconds she proceeded to yell every affirmative phrase she could. "Yes, baby, right there. That's it. I'm close." I may as well have been in the room with them, her voice couldn't have been clearer. I dropped my head to the table and banged it once. Bring back Mr and Mrs Harris, the elderly couple who were in bed by eight p.m. each night and obviously never had sex.

Were these people deliberately trying to ruin me tonight? I'd been polite about the music. I hadn't called the cops, though I surely could have. What time did noise restrictions begin? I didn't know, but surely it was before eleven p.m. And now they were going to have the worlds noisiest sex. The graze on my arm throbbed. My internet was out again. And I still hadn't called my damn sister.

Frig this.

Frig them.

Frig everything.

I shoved myself back from the table, not caring that I knocked the chair over in the process and stormed across the room. I curled my fingers into fists, and blood rushed in my ears. Inconsiderate assholes. I'd tell them exactly what I thought of their shit taste in music and their overdone, porn-style moaning.

As if Dr Porn Star Wannabe was *that* great in bed.

I raised my fist to thump on the wall as another woman's voice joined the first. My eyes widened, and my hand froze. Was he having an…orgy? Maybe it wasn't a housewarming party, but a sex party? Holy wow.

I shook my head. Even more reason to tell them off. This was a nice, family area. I could have had young children in here for all they knew. I readied my arm, prepared to beat down the wall and yell every obscenity I could think of, when I heard the voice of my anger management coach in my head, asking me if I really needed to react with anger over this. Had I tried everything in my power to resolve this calmly and rationally?

I almost stomped my foot, but she would have frowned on that, too. Shit. I probably hadn't. He'd turned down the music when I'd asked. Maybe I should go over and politely ask if they could put a pillow over her head when she came. Or something. That's what normal people would do, wouldn't they?

Or… They'd just ignore it.

An incessant little voice in my head taunted that maybe I was so ticked off because I hadn't had sex in almost a year. Self-imposed sex ban or not, it's not like I didn't have the same primal urges as every other twenty-something female. I slunk back to the table as one of the women next door had, what sounded like, a mind-shattering orgasm. I breathed deeply. Good. For. Her.

I tried to mean it. I really did. I clicked through the website and got the *Internet not connected* page again. I clenched my fingers but forced each one to relax as I waited for the Wi-Fi reconnect pop-up. I hovered the mouse over my network, neatly labelled with my first initial and surname, when I realised there was a new network available to join.

Damien's House of Debauchery.

Moaner number two started up again, making me roll my eyes. I right-clicked on my own network and navigated to the settings.

With a small, smug smile on my face, I changed the network name to *I can hear you having sex.*

Unless their Wi-Fi was a shitty as mine was, they probably wouldn't even notice. But the small act of defiance made me feel better. I hadn't lost my cool. I was still on the reinvention of Bree wagon, but I never claimed to be a saint. I gave up studying and crawled into bed. I fell asleep to the not so dulcet tones of a bedframe hitting the wall.

3

BREE

The shrill beeping of my alarm pierced through the fog of sleep. Five a.m. Blah. My eyes were as scratchy as sandpaper and my body a dead weight. Being conscious right now was deeply unwelcome. But I had a morning routine and I needed to keep it. Especially after the way I'd almost, if not completely, fallen off the cool, calm, and collected bandwagon yesterday.

I cringed at how many times I'd lost my temper. First with Dr Guzman, then with Dr Can't Ride a Bike, then with his porno co-stars. I scrubbed a hand over my face. In the space of one day, I'd almost managed to undo a whole year worth of good.

But today was a new day. I wasn't perfect, and learning to control my temper and become a better person was a step-by-step process. And the first step was morning yoga. I'd been doing daily YouTube videos and I liked the way it set up my day. Strong. Positive. Focused.

But after I pulled on some workout clothes and unrolled my yoga mat in front of the TV, the YouTube app wouldn't open. Because, of course, the blinking internet was out.

I clenched my jaw but then forcibly relaxed it. I'd buy a new router today. That was the solution. Not getting pissed off. *Just reconnect the internet and carry on with your day, Bree.*

The available network connections popped up, the first one mine, still labelled *I can hear you having sex.* I couldn't believe I'd done that. So passive-aggressive. I vowed to change it as soon as I was done with this workout.

I was just about to connect when I noticed the name of the network beneath mine. Last night it had been called *Damien's House of Debauchery.* Right now, it was simply called *Jealous?*

My face went hot. Well, that was embarrassing.

Ugh. Should I go over there and explain? I wondered what Dr Guzman would suggest, but after a moment of pondering, I vowed to just get on with my workout and worry about the new neighbours later. Maybe I'd get lucky and never have to see them face to face. A girl could hope.

Yoga was good for clearing the mind, and I managed a quick cram session while I ate a hastily put-together omelette. My bike helmet, slightly dinged from my stack yesterday, sat on the table, and I picked it up on my way out. I was still fumbling with my keys, trying to get the screen door to lock when the door next to mine opened.

I froze as a tall brunette woman and a shorter, curvier blonde tumbled into the hall, laughing. They were the same two women who had been singing when I'd stomped over there last night.

They kissed, linking their fingers together, then turned back to the doorway where Dr Half Naked stood in nothing but low-slung sleep pants. "See you tonight, Damien."

My mouth dropped open as they both kissed him on the cheek then giggled their way down the hall. He leant on the doorframe, watching them go, not noticing I was there.

"It's too early in the morning for this," I mumbled under my breath.

He started at my voice, then folded his arms across his bare chest. A really frigging nice chest it was, too. Black and grey tattoos circled his pecs and travelled down one arm. I hadn't expected the body art. They didn't exactly fit the clean-cut doctor stereotype, but they certainly made my mouth water. And those abs I'd caught a glimpse of last night...well, in full, they could probably cut—

He coughed, and I snapped my attention back to his smug grin. Silence drew out between us while his gaze roved over me from head to toe then back up again.

The guy had just sent two women on a walk of shame and no less than thirty seconds later, he was leering at me. He had stamina, I'd give him that.

"So, are you?" he asked as I finally wrestled my screen door into submission.

"Am I what?"

His smirk morphed into a grin. "Jealous?"

To my mortification my face burned, and I knew I was blushing. I shot him a dirty look and stormed past him towards the elevator. His laughter followed me. "Oh, come on. I was only joking. And you started it!"

I ignored him, choosing to bypass the elevator. The stairs would be quicker. I flung open the exit and didn't look back. Of all the men, in all the world, did it have to be him who had moved in next door? So much for starting my day out right. Ugh.

I'D STOMPED the length of the block before I realised I'd completely bypassed my bike, chained at the front of our building. Oh well. I didn't dare go back for it, in case I ran into him again. And anyway, walking seemed like a better option.

I still hadn't rung my sister.

And I needed to. I'd promised Dr Guzman I'd do it yesterday, and it was gnawing away at me. The not knowing what she'd say was more distracting than I could afford when I had my first exam in an hour. And there'd been too much losing my temper in the last twenty-four hours. I needed to push forward, not roll back. I pulled my phone from my bag and rang the last number I'd had for her, hoping it was still right.

My sister and I had been close as kids. She was only two years older, but it had been her bed I'd crawled into at night when I'd had nightmares. It was her shoulder I'd cried on when kids at school had picked on me because I'd been a bit of an ugly duckling. It had been her I'd gushed to when Tim, the boy I'd been crushing on for six months, asked me out. Once upon a time, I could have never imagined anything coming between us. But I'd also never imagined she'd run off with my high school sweetheart. Then marry him. Leaving me with no boyfriend. No best friend. No sister.

The call tone trilled in my ear as I held my breath, not sure whether I wanted it to be the right number or not. Then a cautious, "Hello?"

I stopped walking, my mind going completely blank at her voice. It was her. She still had the same number, even after all these years. I closed my eyes.

"Is anyone there?"

Was I really doing this? Was I really going to confront the woman who'd run off with the man I'd loved? The man I'd once thought I'd marry? Tim and I had been together from age sixteen to eighteen. Then they'd begun sneaking around behind my back. It had been several years since I'd spoken to either of them. Not since the day I'd found out about them. "Yes," I answered quietly. "I'm here."

There was a sharp intake of breath on the other end. "Bree?"

I nodded. Then realising that was ridiculous, confirmed. "Yes. Hi, Lou." Just like that, I'd slipped into my childhood nickname for her. I couldn't help it. Old habits die hard.

"How...how are you?"

I plastered a smile and tried to force some enthusiasm into

my voice. "I'm fine. I'm good. I've got my own place in Sydney, and I'm working on a film set doing hair and makeup. And I'm studying, too. I'm doing really great, actually. How are you? How's… Tim?"

She paused for a moment, and when she did answer, her voice was quiet. "He's good."

I nodded again. I really had to stop doing that. "That's good." Wow. This conversation was going well. Lou seemed to come to the same conclusion and changed the subject.

"Do you have time to talk? I could meet you somewhere, for coffee? Just name a place and I'll get there."

Whoa. Of all the ways I thought this would play out, her asking me out for coffee was not one of them. "Uh, no. Sorry. I have an exam in an hour. I just called to say…actually I don't know what I called to say. I just called."

"I want to talk to you. I've wanted to call you so many times, but I just never knew what the right thing to do was. I didn't want to hurt you more than we already had."

Something twisted inside me. Something I'd long buried because it had once hurt so badly it had nearly destroyed me. Lou and Tim had been the two people closest to me, and they'd betrayed me in the worst way possible. They couldn't hurt me more than they already had.

"I can't do coffee. I really do have an exam."

"Dinner then? Saturday night? Come to our place. I'll cook, and we can catch up."

I bit my lip. It was one thing for me to call her, and to speak to her briefly on the phone. But to see her face to face? To see them together? No.

"I don't think so, Lou."

"Please? I know there's a lot of bad blood between us. But you called me. There must be some little part of you that wants to work this out? Please. Just give me a chance to explain. Come for dinner."

I sighed. I could practically hear Dr Guzman jumping up and down on her lounge with pom poms, encouraging me to go. "Okay. Dinner would be…nice."

It probably wouldn't be. How the hell was I supposed to sit across the table from my sister and my ex and watch them play happy families while I sat on the other side, alone and pathetic? The woman they'd screwed over, still a spinster. They'd probably be able to tell I hadn't had so much as a kiss in the past year.

No. That wasn't going to happen. If I was going to go to dinner, I wasn't going as some pathetic loser.

I needed a date.

4

DAMIEN

"What are you grinning about?"

I stacked a pile of papers, tapping the edges on the reception desk to align them all before I turned said grin on Cleo. She pulled her headset off her ear and raised a knowing eyebrow at me.

"What? I'm not grinning."

"You look like the cat that got the cream."

I laughed and shook my head but leant in a little closer so the patients in the waiting room behind me wouldn't hear. "I'm trying to think up ways to impress a woman I met."

"You met someone?" She gave me a genuine smile. "Damien, that's great. What's her name?"

I opened my mouth to answer, but nothing came out. I wracked my brain. "You know what? I've no idea."

"What do you mean? Did you have a one-night stand?" she hissed. "That's not like you. You love having a girlfriend. But it has been ages since you broke up with Cassidy. I could understand…"

I shook my head. "No, no. Nothing like that." Though she was right. It had been ages since Cass and I had broken up, and my hand was getting pretty boring. It wasn't like I hadn't been look-ing, but no one had even remotely piqued my interest. Until yesterday when I'd crashed into a hot blonde, and then later when I realised she was my neighbour.

"You look like shit this morning. You sure you weren't up all night, making some poor woman scream?"

"Thank you for those kind words. But no. Unfortunately, it wasn't me making women scream last night. Jess, on the other hand…"

"Oh." Cleo gave me an understanding nod. "That's right. Millie got back from France yesterday, didn't she? She and Jess must have been happy to see one another after three months apart."

I flicked the lid off a pen and scribbled on a form that was marked for my signature. "Happy is an understatement. We had a few friends over for a housewarming party, and the two of them snuck off to bed before everyone had even left. Then kept me awake all night with the world's loudest sex."

Cleo patted my shoulder sarcastically. "I'd feel sorry for you, but I like Jess more than you, so good for her."

I clutched my heart dramatically as she shoved another stack of papers my way, pointing at the places I needed to sign. "Any-way, it's tough luck for you if you're tired this morning. You need to look alive. Doctor Simpson from head office is here for the next two weeks, remember?"

I grimaced. I hadn't remembered. "Shit. Really? Is he already here?"

She nodded.

"You couldn't have told me that before I stood here gossiping with you about my roommate's sex life?"

She shrugged. "Hey, you're my boss. Not the other way around." Then she winked at me, because we both knew who really ruled the roost around here. And it wasn't me.

"Your first patient of the day is a Mrs Braun. She's new. Hopefully she's a super rare or interesting case you can use to impress them. I heard a rumour they're looking at you for a promotion."

I'd swear the woman knew everything that happened around here. "That so?" I loved my job, but I also hoped Mrs Braun was just a run-of-the-mill case, with nothing too problematic going on. For her sake. I turned to the waiting room and called loudly so all the patients would hear. "Mrs Braun?"

A woman, in her mid-twenties perhaps, stood and smiled nervously. I indicated to the office on my left, holding the door open for her, then closed it behind me. At my desk, I settled into my chair, and she took one of the facing seats. It wasn't completely unusual for a woman to come in for a first consultation on her own, but most came with their partners, so I was curious.

"I have your referral here," I began, smiling warmly at her. The woman looked so nervous she might puke. I hoped not. Despite being a doctor, I hated vomit. "But I'd rather just hear from you. What can I help you with?"

She took in a shaky breath. "I want a baby."

She'd come to the right place. Making babies is what I did. I hated that I couldn't help every patient I saw, but I was good at my job and I'd helped a lot of families conceive. I had a wall full of baby photos behind me to prove it. "And you've been trying but nothing is happening?"

She nodded.

"For how long?"

She lowered her eyes. "Five years."

I tried to keep the surprise from my face. "Five? And this is the first time you've sought medical help? May I ask why?"

She sighed. "At first, we weren't really trying properly, you know? Just not preventing. So I didn't think much of it. But over the last few years, it's been a different story. I've tried everything. Ovulation sticks. Different diets. Charting my cycle. Nothing helps. I wanted to come earlier, but my husband…"

"He didn't want to come?"

She shrugged. "He doesn't like talking about it. He wants a baby so badly, but each month nothing happens, it's like he takes it personally."

It wasn't an uncommon reaction in men. They often buried their heads in the sand, preferring to ignore any potential problem with their reproductive system, rather than come in and talk about it. Their biological clock often didn't tick as loud as their partner's. Mrs Braun twisted her hands nervously in her lap, waiting on my reply.

"I understand. How about I order some tests for you first, and we take it from there?"

She nodded, her ponytail bouncing up and down. "Thank you. That would be great."

I typed up the necessary paperwork, printed it, and walked around the table to hand it to her. As I opened the door, I patted her reassuringly on the shoulder. "We'll get to the bottom of the problem. I can't promise a baby, but I can promise I'll do everything I can to make it happen."

Her bottom lip trembled as she thanked me. Over her shoulder, Dr Simpson from head office looked up from where he was drinking coffee while reading the paper. He nodded at me approvingly, as if being polite to my patient was something to be commended. Weird. But hey, if he wanted to give me Brownie points for just doing my job, I wouldn't complain. The promotion rumour that had been circling the practice hadn't been lost on me.

I wanted it.

I also wanted the blonde living in the next apartment. And I needed to come up with a way of impressing her. ASAP.

The doctors from head office wanted to go for a drink as soon as the practice closed, so it was almost eight by the time I unlocked my bike and began riding home. I still hadn't come up with a way of impressing my new neighbour, and it was all I could think about. I wanted to see her. Tonight. But I couldn't just rock up there for no reason. I had to come up with something that would show her that I wasn't always a cocky bastard. Sometimes I could even be a little bit charming.

The smell of fresh, hot pizza drifted by as I passed a local Italian place and I hit the brakes, skidding to a stop.

I'd just realised how to get the girl.

5

DAMIEN

I took the stairs two at a time to our fourth-floor apartment, and crashed through the door, impatient to get my plan underway. The pizza wasn't getting any warmer after all.

Jess and Millie looked up from where they were making out on the lounge. "You're late," Jess said, eyeing the pizza box. "But you brought dinner, so you're forgiven." She dropped a kiss on Millie's upturned face and wandered over to where I was searching every cupboard and drawer in the kitchen. "What are you looking for?" She opened the pizza box, but I smacked her hand away.

"Hey! What's that about?"

"Ha!" I yelled as I came up triumphant, brandishing a permanent marker I'd found in an unpacked box on the kitchen floor. I uncapped it, opened the pizza box, and began scrawling text across the inside lid.

Jess came around my side of the kitchen bench and laughed at what she read over my shoulder. "So, you're going after the sour puss next door?"

"He's doing what?" Millie yelled from the lounge, springing up to come study my artwork. She laughed, too.

"Think it'll work?"

Jess squinted at me as Millie wrapped her arms around her middle, resting her chin on Jess' shoulder. "I don't know. She looked pretty pissed last night. And this morning. What did you do to her anyway?"

"Nothing." Then I scrunched up my face. "Besides maybe accidentally knocking her off her bike." There was that unfortunate incident. And then I'd asked her out, and she'd rejected me. And then I'd laughed at her as she'd been leaving her apartment this morning. She hadn't seemed too happy about that either…

Jess punched me in the arm. "Damien!"

I shrugged. "I didn't mean to!"

Millie rolled her eyes. "You've got Buckley's chance, mate, but I want to see how this plays out. So go on. Get over there."

"You think?"

Jess nodded. "She probably already hates you. You can't make it worse. What's her name anyway?"

"I really wish everyone would stop asking me that."

Millie shoved the pizza box in my hand and pushed me out the door. "For Christ's sake. Go. And don't forget to ask her name, ay?"

I shuffled over to the door the gorgeous blonde had come out of this morning and knocked, shooting a quick thumbs-up to Millie and Jess when movement sounded from inside the apartment. Jess and Millie, who had their heads poking out the door, grinned back. Jess mimed eating popcorn, and I stifled a laugh.

I opened the pizza box so it covered my face as the lock clicked. The door opened, and for a moment there was only silence. Then she read out my words. "Would it be too cheesy if I asked you to have dinner with me?"

I dropped the pizza lid and gave the woman standing there my most charming smile. "Would it?"

She scowled at me in return. Right. Well. This was a good start. She shoved her hands on her hips. Shit. She was mad.

"Is this a prank?" she fumed.

I glanced over at Jess and Millie, whose eyes were wide, before I snapped my head back to face her. The woman stepped out of her apartment, forcing me backwards into the hall and swung her head from side to side as if she were searching for hidden cameras or Ashton Kutcher to jump out and yell *punked*!

Jess and Mille pulled their heads inside just in time to avoid the woman's glare. Me, however, not so fortunate.

She turned back to me, fury in her eyes. "This isn't funny."

She tried to slam the door, but I caught it. "Wait. Stop." I dropped all traces of charming grins and turned serious. "I'm not pranking you and I'm not trying to be funny. I have this whole pizza and I thought you might like to share it with me. Honestly. No hidden agendas."

Her gaze turned sceptical, but a little of her fire died, and it spurred me on. "It's double cheese, meatlovers with stuffed crust? It's good. I swear."

"Not if you're vegetarian."

My face fell. "You're vegetarian?" Damn. So much for this brilliant plan. I hadn't even considered that.

The tiniest of smiles pulled at the corner of her mouth. "No. But I could have been."

Relief flooded me, and I realised how much I'd honestly wanted her to agree to this. Something about her intrigued me, and the fact she kept knocking me back and beating me down with her words only made me want to get to know her more. I'm sure one of the shrinks in the complex at work would diagnose self-destructive behaviour because she looked like the sort of woman who could make me cry, but damn. I wanted to know her anyway.

"Since you do like to eat dead animals, at least on occasion, do you want to do that with me tonight? It's a big pizza."

She cocked her head to the side. Then opened the door wider. "Fine. Come in. But just so you know, I'm only agreeing to this because I haven't had dinner and that pizza smells so good I'd sell my firstborn child to eat it. This isn't a date. Because I already told you, I don't do those right now."

"I'll take that."

She pointed to a little round table that sat off the side of her kitchen. A fat grey cat watched me from the windowsill on the other side of the room. "Cute cat."

"Not really. She hates everyone but me and she has the potential to claw your eyes out. It's not a great combination."

The fluffball hissed from her perch on the windowsill, as if to accentuate the point, and I edged around the table away from her.

"Thanks for the warning." I wondered if the cat's owner possessed similar qualities. She seemed the type to bite. Though in the right setting, I wasn't completely opposed to that.

We settled in chairs next to each other, and both of us grabbed a slice.

"So, uh, this is awkward, but I don't even know your name." Then I tacked on, "I'm Damien, by the way."

She paused with her slice in midair. "Yes, I know your name, Doctor Damien of Damien's House of Debauchery. I saw it on your name tag yesterday. I'm Bree."

"Pretty name."

"Thank you. Can I eat this now?"

"Sure."

We ate in silence as I glanced around the neat apartment. The layout was identical to the place I shared with Jess. Kitchen by the door flowing into a living area. Bedrooms and a bathroom off to the right of the room. I spied a pile of text books on the edge of the kitchen bench and twisted to read the spines.

"Naturopathy?"

She bristled, as if I'd offended her. I had no idea how, though. My presence in general seemed to offend her.

"Yes. I just started."

I nodded as I leant across and plucked one from the pile to flick through it. "That's awesome. Good for you."

She stared.

"What? Do I have food on my face?"

"No, I just…do you mean that?"

"Mean what?"

"You don't think naturopathy is some fake, hippy crap that really has no benefit to anyone?"

"Uh, no. Is that what you think?"

She wiped her fingers on a napkin before placing it back on the table. "Of course not. But you're a doctor. And most doctors think naturopathy is ridiculous."

"Most doctors are old-school. I've only been qualified a few years. I like to think I'm not old-school yet." I smiled at her, now understanding some of her prickliness towards me. "I think there's a lot of good that can come from natural healing. I use some of it at my practice. And I regularly refer my patients to holistic healers before we try more invasive procedures."

Her posture softened. "I'm sorry. I'm always having to defend myself in one way or another. It's nice to not be laughed at. Most people think it's a load of rubbish."

I sat back in my chair, dead serious. "Well, I don't."

She gave a tiny nod. "I had my first exam today. I think I failed it, though."

"Why would you think that?"

She shrugged then rolled her eyes at me. "I didn't get to study as much as I wanted. Some jackass doctor knocked me off my bike."

"The jackass doctor is still really sorry about that. Is your arm okay?"

She waved a hand. "It's fine. It wasn't just the arm that made studying difficult. It was more the fact I couldn't study while you were having the world's loudest threesome."

I choked on my pizza and had to take a sip of my drink before I could answer. Her expression was smug, like she knew exactly who and what I was, and I couldn't help laughing. "You think I had a threesome last night?"

Her smile faded. "Well, didn't you? I saw those women leave your apartment this morning."

I shook my head. The thought of Millie, Jess, and me having a threesome was too hysterical to comprehend. Jess had been my best friend since we were eleven. Even back then, we'd both known she wasn't into guys. We'd lived together all through university and my residency. She'd met Millie six months ago, and the two of them had been tight ever since. It had nearly killed Jess when Millie had gone to France for three months on a work trip.

"That was my roommate and her girlfriend."

Bree's mouth formed at little round O, which fascinated me. Her lips were a delicious pink colour and naturally plump. I suddenly found myself wondering how they'd feel against mine. I cleared my throat. "I'm somewhat proud you thought I had enough game to pull two women, though. I feel like I should thank you for that, but the truth is, I'm nowhere near that cool."

Bree leant her elbows on the table. "In that case, could you let them know how thin the walls are here? It was like being on a porn set last night."

I picked up another piece of pizza. "Don't worry, I had to hear it all, too. They've already had a talking to and have promised to keep it down in future."

She nodded and reached out to thumb through the text book I'd left on the table. It made me remember that she'd said she thought she'd failed her exam. "Maybe I can help you study sometime?"

She looked up, surprise written all over her features. "Why

would you want to do that? Surely you're pretty sick of studying by the time you get a doctor's degree."

"I feel bad. The bike. The party. Millie and Jess's theatrics. Let me help make it up to you."

Her expression changed, as if something had only just occurred to her. But with my eyes on her lips, I didn't get a chance to analyse what she might be thinking. I inched closer. She really was pretty. Not just her mouth either. Her high cheekbones and perfectly shaped eyebrows and all that golden hair falling around her face.

"I don't need study help, but there is something else you could help me with…"

"Name it."

"It's going to sound weird."

"Okayyy," I said slowly.

"I need a date."

I quirked an eyebrow. "You said you don't date. Though, we're already on one. Sort of."

She ignored my deliberate needling. "I need a date for a family dinner. And not just a date. I kind of need…a boyfriend."

"A what now?"

"You heard me."

"I heard you say you want me to be your boyfriend. Maybe buy me dinner first? Geez, I feel so used." I grinned at her, and she rolled her eyes but she was laughing. And fuck me. If I'd thought her pretty when she smiled, she was fucking stunning when she laughed. Straight white teeth between those pink lips. Her cheeks rosy, her eyes crinkling slightly in the corners. Laughing Bree nearly knocked me off my chair.

"So, will you?"

"Will I what?" I'd lost all train of thought. My brain was short-circuiting.

"Will you come to dinner at my sister's house and pretend to be my boyfriend."

"That depends. I have a counter offer."

"Is this a negotiation?"

"Maybe. I'll be your fake date if you'll be mine."

"You need a fake date." The look on her face was pure scepticism. "That's convenient."

She had a point. But the more I thought about it, the more this plan seemed like a good idea. "I have a little work dinner on Friday night and I'm up for a promotion. There's a lot of people there I want to impress. And showing up with you on my arm would be impressive."

She tapped her painted fingernails on the table while she mulled over my offer. And I found myself holding my breath, hoping she'd say yes. She was an impressive woman, I'd meant that. She was tall and blonde and hot as fuck, but beyond that, I liked the way she didn't take bullshit. She wasn't afraid to put me in my place. She had an exterior that very well may have been made of stone, but damn if I didn't love a challenge. It was why I'd gone into medicine. Was there anything more complicated than the human body and all the millions of things that could go wrong with it? I loved the daily puzzle of trying to fix people. And Bree's external barriers had to be sheltering something soft. There had to be a reason she had walls up.

"I kind of hate doctors."

"You don't hate me."

"Don't I?"

I leant forward so I was only inches from her face. I'd almost expected her to sit back, but she didn't even blink. Just stared right back at me as if she knew all my moves. Maybe she did.

"You might want to hate me, but you don't. I'm wearing down your barriers every moment we sit here." I had no idea if that was true. But I was willing to call her bluff. And I found myself wanting it to be true. I wanted to get under her skin.

She leant in even closer and bit her bottom lip. Holy shit. My heart hammered. I wanted to close the gap completely. I wanted to taste her and find out if those lips were as soft as they looked. A tiny smile pulled at the corner of her mouth.

"You wish," she said before she sat back in her chair and crossed her arms over her chest with a laugh.

I blinked. Shit. She was possibly better at this game than I was. I needed to turn it up a notch.

"Fine. A date for a date. Purely a business arrangement." She stuck her hand out for me to shake. "Deal?"

As if no was even an option. "Hell. Yes. Do I get to kiss you? You know, for appearance's sake only. Of course."

She huffed, but I couldn't help riling her up. It was too much fun. "You do know this is just a fake date, right? Fake. As in, I'm not going anywhere near your dick."

I half coughed, half laughed. Feisty was the understatement of the century. "Much to my dick's disgust, I can deal with that. I'll be the perfect fake boyfriend. I'll make small talk with your sister and keep my hands to myself at all times. I promise."

I took her hand, ignoring the sparks shooting up my arm from her touch, and shook on it. But then I winked at her. Because really, I wasn't sure that was a promise I wanted to keep.

6

———————

BREE

*S*ydney Harbour glinted in the early evening light, and the docked boats bobbed on the water. My heels clicked off the cement paths as I strolled to the restaurant. I'd insisted on meeting Damien at his work dinner, since he was going for pre-dinner drinks and I'd had to work until five p.m., then rush home to get ready. After he filled me in on the details, I realised his 'little' work dinner was actually a function for almost a hundred people in a booked-out restaurant called La Mer. It sat right on the water's edge, and I could only imagine how much a function for one hundred people would cost. But they were doctors, so I supposed they weren't short of coin.

I paused outside the door to the restaurant, my hand hovering over the silver door handle as an uncomfortable feeling spread across my chest. I'd almost died when Damien had told me the name of the restaurant.

I'd been here once before. About a year ago with a man I'd been married to for five minutes. After my sister and Tim had run off, I'd bounced from one relationship to another until a man named Rick had pursued me. Our marriage had been doomed from the start.

I cringed at the memory of that night. I'd made a huge scene and said some horrible things that I was so ashamed of. I hated even thinking about that time in my life, because every time I did, I sunk into the feelings of guilt and shame, and it was hard to pull myself back out. I'd worked hard so I wouldn't have to carry around those negative feelings for life. Taking a deep breath, I straightened my shoulders. I wasn't going to get sucked down that vortex tonight because I wasn't that person any more. People could change.

Inside the restaurant, a waitress showed me to where the function was being held, and I scanned the busy room for Damien. Several long tables filled the space, each with flower centrepieces. The lighting was dim, and low jazz music played over the speakers, giving the room a cosy, intimate feel, despite the large number of people there. People—doctors I presumed —milled around with drinks in their hands, smiling and nodding, talking in groups. Through the crowd, I spotted Damien, a pair of black-framed glasses giving him a Clark Kent vibe. He spoke around an animated smile, using his hands for emphasis, with his tie loosened and shirt sleeves rolled up to the elbow. My gaze traced the intricate pattern of tattoos on his arm, and I found myself wanting to know exactly how many he had.

A little part of me wasn't ashamed to admit I wouldn't mind finding out firsthand.

I'd committed to my twelve-month celibacy stint, and I only had a few weeks left on it, so I wanted to see it out. But eleven months without sex was suddenly feeling like a long time. And being out tonight, in the same vicinity as a man I was clearly attracted to, even if he was a sometimes a dickwad, was not going to help matters. I had a feeling tonight was going to be a struggle, and not because I'd have to make small talk with a roomful of people I didn't know. I took a wineglass from a passing waiter and navigated the crowd to his side. "Hey."

He turned at my voice, his eyes widening when he realised it was me. "Wow. I mean, hi."

His gaze swept over me slowly, and I wasn't surprised to find it warmed my skin. I'd worn heels and a full-length black jumpsuit that showed off my long legs. Plus, I'd taken the time to curl my hair, pleased that it was finally a length I could do something with. It fell in waves around my shoulders. I knew I looked good, but damn, he was no slouch either. I'd give him that. His hair was messed up just enough to be sexy, the stubble on his jaw deliberate. The glasses, combined with the tats and the muscled forearms? Yeah, the entire package was doing it for me.

Shit. I might be in trouble here.

I raised an eyebrow, pretending I wasn't checking him out. His hazel eyes were slightly glassy, and I suspected the bourbon in his hand wasn't his first. "I didn't realise you wore glasses." Frig. I was practically purring.

"I wear contacts most of the time. The glasses only come out for special occasions."

"I like them. Want to introduce me to your friends?"

He started, as if he'd perhaps forgotten there was a group of people watching us curiously. "Right. Of course." He took my hand in his and turned back to the group. "Everyone, this is Bree. My date. Bree, this is Dr Alexander Simpson, Dr Susan Michelson…"

He went around the circle, introducing each person, all of them doctors, but I zoned out, distracted by the feel of my hand in his. His hand was large and tan, and his skin against mine sent pleasurable little waves through my body. Jesus. If just holding his hand was doing things to me, imagine if he touched me elsewhere—

"Bree?"

I suddenly realised the entire group were staring at me.

"Excuse me, sorry. What was the question?"

The man next to me, Alex his name was, answered, "I asked

what you do for work?" His breath reeked of alcohol, and he'd directed his question to my cleavage.

"Oh. I'm a makeup artist." I smiled at him, trying not to focus on the fact his eyebrows met in the middle. I could fix those up quick smart if I had my gear with me.

"She's studying naturopathy as well. She just aced her first exam," Damien added on, winking at me.

I wouldn't find out if I'd aced the exam for weeks yet, but still, it was nice of him to say that. I was still freaking out over potentially failing.

"So, you do all that waxing and laser stuff?" Alex asked, his nose crinkling slightly. "I don't know how you can stand it. Though, I suppose, you and Damien have that in common. Working in the downstairs area each day." His laugh echoed around the group, and he leant over to thump Damien on the back.

Damien squeezed my hand lightly, and I forced a smile. The man hadn't even listened to me. Or he somehow thought that beautician and makeup artist was the same thing. Did he just assume that all us blonde bimbos with boobs did the same thing? That was frigging rude. And degrading. I couldn't hold my tongue. "It's no big deal. Just part of the job. When the guys come in for back, sack, and crack waxes, that's my favourite," I snapped in an over exaggerated Australian accent while I glanced at the man's crotch.

Alex choked on his drink, and Damien snorted. My cheeks went hot. Seriously. My mouth. Why had I said that? I wasn't going to be any help to Damien tonight if I couldn't at least pretend to be classy. In fact, he'd probably ask me to leave before I had a go at any more of his colleagues.

"Your attention, please?" a waiter called from the side of the room, and I was grateful for the distraction. "Dinner will be served in a moment, so if you could all take your seats."

Damien tugged on my hand, leading me towards the end of one of the long tables.

"We should sit in the middle," I hissed at him. "So you can network? You're only going to get to talk to me all the way down here."

"I know. Why do you think I'm heading in this direction? Alex isn't the only dickhead in this room."

Oh. That was…really kind of charming, and I had to admit, I liked the idea of spending the dinner at the quiet end of the table with his attention on me. But it wasn't what I was here for. "Fake date, Damien," I reminded him. Fake date. Celibacy vow. I perhaps needed them written on flash cards so I could remind myself of both while he kept saying all the right things.

"Yeah, but this one is my fake date, so I call the shots. You can call the shots tomorrow when I'm your fake boyfriend. Deal?"

I couldn't help the tiny grin that escaped me. "Fine. Boss."

Something sparked in his eyes, making me wish he'd say whatever it was he was thinking. I had a feeling it may not be appropriate for the company we were keeping. He pulled my chair out for me before settling into his own.

"So, since this is your night, how 'bout you tell me why it is you need a fake date? You're a young, good-looking doctor." I let my gaze drop to his arm that rested on the tabletop. "With tattoos. You should have women beating down your door."

Seriously. What was wrong with the guy? He had a vibe going on right now that I was more into by the moment. I couldn't be the only one.

"I like relationships." He sat back as a waitress placed meals in front of each of us, but he leant back in as soon as we'd thanked her. "I haven't been in one for a while, and I don't have time for clubs or pubs or hookup apps. So, no. I don't have women beating down my door. Except you."

"I didn't beat down your door," I protested.

"Fine. I don't have women knocking loudly on my door, except for you."

I snickered. "So, you're a workaholic?"

"Depends on your definition. I work more set hours now that I'm working in fertility. But there's still a lot of study involved outside of work and a lot of work functions I'm required to attend. Some women don't like that." He shrugged. "But what's your story? I'm not the only one who needed a fake date. You're hot as fuck. Why aren't you taken?"

I hoped I was wearing enough makeup to cover the blush that was no doubt staining my cheeks. "Thanks. I think?" I laughed, hoping he wouldn't press me on my reasons, but he just waited quietly, those eyes trained on mine in the dim light, not at all concerned we were effectively ignoring all of his colleagues and the food in front of us. I sighed.

"You really want to know? It's long and ugly."

"Nothing about you could be ugly."

Ha. He didn't know me at all. Didn't have a clue about all the horrible things I'd done and said. All the people I'd hurt. "I was married. Not that long ago. His name is Rick."

"So, I'm the rebound guy?"

"Ha, no. I think he was actually. Maybe all my relationships have been rebounds, in one way or another. Our marriage only lasted a short time. Like, we're talking a few weeks. The whole thing was a train wreck. He was married when we got together. I didn't know at the time, and by the time I did find out I was too far gone to care. He left her. For me. Then dumped me on my ass to go back to her."

To Damien's credit, he didn't look completely disgusted. Which was kind of him because I was more than disgusted enough with myself for both of us.

"Everyone makes mistakes."

"Mine was a pretty big one."

"Question is, did you learn from it?"

I didn't even need to think about how to answer that. "Yes. I had—no, I still do have anger issues and impulse control problems. Not from him. From something...someone hurt me, a long time ago. Someone I thought would never betray me the way they did. I'm not using that as an excuse because what I did was unforgivable. I was a bitch. I know that. But I've been working hard with a therapist for a year now, trying to better myself. She's the one who said I need to sort things out with my family, hence the dinner tomorrow night. It's all part of me trying to make up for the wrongs I've done and the people I've hurt. Sometimes I think I'm there, and then other days I realise I still have a long way to go. I'm a work in progress."

I sat back in my chair and squinted at him. "Sorry. I don't know why I'm telling you all this. We should talk to your colleagues. I'll try to keep my mouth shut and just look pretty on your arm."

He frowned. "Don't do that."

"What?"

"Sell yourself short. You're more than just a pretty face. This room may be filled with over-privileged doctors, but I didn't invite you here just to be arm candy, Bree. I for one, am completely intrigued by you. You and the skeletons in your closet."

My stomach flipped as he moved closer, his voice low. "Truth is. I didn't actually need a date for this dinner. I've been to a million of these by myself. They're practically a weekly event. I just wanted to get to know you."

Oh.

Fake date was apparently not so fake after all. I should probably be angry, since he'd brought me here on false pretences. But if this was real, judging by the low simmering heat spreading through my blood, my celibacy vow was in trouble. Traitorous damn body.

He cocked his head to the side, mischief twinkling in his eyes.

He seemed completely sober now. "I can tell you want to be angry about that, but you can't, can you? In fact, if I leant in right now and kissed you, I think you'd kiss me back."

So, he'd run me down and had a party? That all seemed like a distant memory, despite the fact it had only been a few days ago and my arm still sported the injury to prove it. But he'd also spent the night complimenting me, and out of scrubs and jeans and t-shirts, he looked damn kissable. If I were being honest, he'd looked kissable in them too, but I'd been too busy flying off the handle to allow myself to think it.

There was nothing in my contract that said I couldn't kiss the guy. "Maybe you should try and see what happens."

He bit his lip and leant in. I let my eyelids flutter closed, the smell of his aftershave and the sweeter scent of the bourbon and Coke wafting around, my toes curling in anticipation. I was dying to know if his kisses were as hot as the promise in his eyes. His stubble brushed my cheek before he whispered in my ear. "Not here. Not yet."

Then he pulled away, leaving me blinking at the sudden loss, wholly unsatisfied, while he sat back and folded his arms across his chest, smug as could be.

I recovered quickly. "It's like that, is it? I'll remember that tomorrow when I'm the boss of the date." If he wanted hard to get, that's what I'd give him. It'd been almost a year since a man had touched me. I could wait. Could he, though? There was sexual chemistry sparking between us, the draw undeniable. One of us would have to release the pressure by giving in at some point.

But it wouldn't be me.

Damien's smile faltered for just the briefest of moments, but I saw it. If he thought he was torturing me tonight, he was in for a world of frustration tomorrow. This was going to be fun.

7

BREE

After our almost kiss at the restaurant, where Damien had made vague promises about 'later' and I'd made smart-ass rebukes about playing hard to get, we'd made more of an effort to speak to the people sitting around us. The pull between us was too great to keep up with the intimate talk and not be able to take it further.

The couple across from us turned out to be nice people from Damien's Melbourne office, who'd chatted with me curiously about naturopathy. Their genuine interest had been the complete opposite of the way Damien's colleague Alex had spoken to me earlier in the evening, and we'd had a great time discussing the merits of various practises. I'd felt comfortable sitting beside Damien with his arm draped loosely over the back of the chair, and afterwards, we'd caught an Uber back to our building.

"Stairs or elevator?" Damien asked as we entered the lobby.

"Elevator. These heels aren't made for stair climbing."

He pushed the button on the wall. And then, while we waited, standing side by side, staring at the elevator doors, his fingers brushed the back of my hand. He slid his hand into mine, and I glanced over at him.

"Is this okay?" he said without looking at me.

I turned back to face the elevator so he wouldn't see the smile on my face.

"It's nice."

The elevator arrived, and the doors whooshed open, revealing an empty space. I followed Damien in and stood beside him. The moment the doors closed, he rounded on me, one hand still linked with mine, pulling me close to his body. I glanced up at him in surprise, my insides turning to lava at the look in his eyes.

"I didn't kiss you in the restaurant tonight because I didn't want our first kiss to be some crappy peck on the lips in front of a room of people. I don't want to kiss you like that, Bree." His voice had turned deep and husky. Sexy as hell.

All thoughts of playing hard to get flew out of my head as he slid his hands along my sides to my waist. A yearning had opened up deep inside me. It had been so long since I'd been this close to a man, and Damien's scent and the way he'd been nothing but a perfect gentleman all evening was driving me mad.

"How do you want to kiss me then?" I whispered

His lips crashed down on mine, hot and demanding, while his fingers simultaneously gripped my hips and lifted me off the floor. I snaked my arms around his shoulders, finding the back of his head with my fingers as I instinctively wrapped my legs around his waist. My back slammed into the wall of the elevator, my head cracking on the polished mirrors, but I didn't care. His tongue ran the seam of my lips, and I opened for him, a moan escaping me when his soft tongue tangled with mine, and something much, much harder pressed between my legs.

The elevator bell dinged, signalling we'd reached our floor, but neither of us stopped. He ground against me, his kiss making me hot all over. I ripped my head away from his lips to gasp, "Doors!" as they began to close. He shot a hand out, while supporting my weight with the other and the pressure of his body. I gripped him like a monkey as he found my lips again and walked us down the hall, past his apartment to my own. My feet slid to the floor, but I couldn't bring myself to stop the kiss. His lips were warm, and our tongues moved in unison, our fingers roaming each other's bodies. It was a long time before I pulled away, breathless, his shirt half undone. I hadn't even realised I'd been undoing it. In the middle of the hallway.

"Fuck," he muttered, stepping back from me, breathing hard with his eyes slightly unfocused. He ran a hand through his hair before shaking his head, a grin spreading across his face.

I leant back on my door and laughed. Fuck indeed.

"That was some kiss."

I bit my lip. It was. And it was only a first kiss. I wasn't sure I'd ever been kissed like that in my life. I could only imagine how he'd kiss me once we'd had some practice together. And how it would feel to have his lips on other parts of my body… We stared at each other for a long moment while I fought with myself. This was where I was supposed to invite him in for coffee or a night-cap. Or as anyone under eighty knew, sex.

"I have to tell you something," I confessed.

He waited.

"First. Stop looking at me like you want to devour me."

"I do, though."

Frig. That was hot. But… "That's not helpful. Because the second thing I need to tell you is that I'm celibate."

"You're what?"

"Celibate. You know, I don't have sex."

His eyes widened. "You're a virgin? Holy shit, I just nearly tried to have sex with a virgin in an elevator. I'm going to Hell. Why didn't you tell me? I would have been more of a gentleman!"

I burst out laughing. "I'm not a virgin. But it has almost been a year. I promised myself I wouldn't for twelve months."

He winced. "I'm afraid to ask how much of that twelve months is left."

"About three weeks."

He closed the gap between us, his hand finding the small of my back and tugging me towards him until my chest hit his. "Thank god for that. Because I don't know how long I can kiss you the way we just did and not want to get you naked. You sure you don't get an early mark for good behaviour?"

I laughed in his hopeful face and tried to fight off the urge to pull him inside. My breasts pressed against his chest, and the friction made me want to rip my shirt off right then and there. "Not tonight. I have a four a.m. on-set start time tomorrow that I'm already going to be late for, considering it's nearly one a.m. now. I should go."

He nodded and brushed his lips over mine again. "Go sleep. But tomorrow…"

"Tomorrow you're my fake date and I call the shots. Remember?"

He groaned. "I'm going to really regret saying that, aren't I?"

"Maybe."

8

BREE

orking on a Saturday morning sucked. But it happened regularly in TV. Certain scenes had to be shot in certain places at certain times of the day, and wherever the cast went, the makeup team went. We were on location this morning, but thankfully we weren't far from home.

I clomped blindly up the stairs of the makeup trailer, five minutes late, with a coffee in each hand. One for now, and one for immediately after. Because a four a.m. start when you'd been up all night thinking about the man in the apartment next door was a recipe for disaster.

A long, low wolf whistle greeted me as I slumped into one of the makeup chairs. "Girl, you look like shit! What the hell were you doing last night? That coffee for me?"

I practically growled at Bianca, and she pulled her hand back, laughing. "Okay, okay, I guess not." She swivelled her chair around so we were face to face instead of talking to each other in the mirrors. She was entirely too chirpy for this time of the morning. I'd met Bianca, or BB as she went by these days, awhile back. She'd worked at a bar with one of my exes, and we'd gone out clubbing a few times together. It had been a surprise when six months ago, I'd found her sitting in my makeup chair, after having nabbed a recurring role on the show. She'd only just begun acting, but even I could tell how good she was. After watching one scene from the side of the set, I'd known exactly why the show had hired a complete newbie for such a big role. She was a natural. And she'd been in my makeup chair every morning since.

I glanced at myself in the mirror. She was right. I looked very average. Tired and makeup-free.

"So, you gonna tell me what you did last night?"

I put my coffee cups down on the bench with a warning look before I began smothering Bianca's cheeks with lotion. "I had a date."

She raised an eyebrow. "But you don't date anymore."

"I know. It was a fake date."

Her brow furrowed.

"That kind of, somehow, turned into a real date."

She clapped, bouncing on her seat. "Was there not fake sex, too? Cos you look like you've been awake all night. Tell me everything."

"Sit still and I will."

I filled her in on all the details of the previous night, laughing at her open mouth when I said I hadn't invited him in.

"So, the celibacy vow. You're still running with that?"

I shrugged. "Close 'em. I need to do your eyes."

She huffed out a sigh and closed her lids so I could apply eyeshadow, but that didn't stop her mouth from running. "I can't believe you had a sexy doctor falling at your feet. A doctor, Bree! With tats and glasses who practically dry humped you in an elevator…"

I let her go on and on with a little smile on my face because reliving last night, through her excitement, wasn't the worst thing in the world. Weirdly, I was already missing Damien. I couldn't stop thinking about the way he'd touched me...the feel of him beneath my hands...

A shadow fell across Bianca's face, and I turned to see what was blocking the light. Only to find Damien leaning on the makeup trailer doorway, holding two steaming coffees. My mouth dropped open.

"What are you doing here?"

"Hey?" Bianca asked, opening her eyes, then doing a double take when she realised I hadn't been speaking to her.

"I brought you coffee," he said, holding one out to me. "Though I see you already have one."

It wasn't even five a.m. and he was only wearing a hoodie with jeans, but damn. I'd spent all night wondering if I'd made up exactly how handsome he was. I hadn't. And now his face had an adorably disappointed expression on it.

"These are mine," Bianca said, pulling both my cups toward her.

"Both of them?"

"Yep." She nodded so vigorously I wondered if she actually had already drunk a few.

"How did you even get on set?" I asked.

Damien turned his attention back to me and chuckled. "I just showed the security guys my ID and told them I was the onset doctor."

"Geez, we need better security around here," I muttered, but I couldn't help grinning at him as I reached to take a coffee.

"Not that one. This one is yours," he said, handing me a tall paper cup with a plastic lid.

I took it, appreciating the steaming warmth. When I lifted it to my mouth, I noticed writing in thick black marker on the side of the cup and paused to read it.

"You are brewtiful," I read out loud. I glanced up at Damien while Bianca made swooning noises from her chair. "You have a thing for puns, huh?" First the pizza box. Now the coffee.

"Depends. Do you like it?"

I didn't hate it. "You may be kind of cute."

He smiled, and something about that smile made me really damn happy. Sure, he did things to my libido, but he was also kind of sweet, bringing me pizza and sneaking onto my set to give me coffee. I was beginning to think this thing between us was something more than smoke and mirrors.

I might have been catching a case of feelings.

"Well, I'll make more of an effort in future then. Cos truthfully, the barista wrote that. I think he might have had a crush on me."

Bianca bust out laughing while Damien grinned. I rolled my eyes, but I couldn't help the laugh that escaped my mouth.

He pushed off the trailer door and crossed the space, leaning down so his lips brushed my ear. "For the record, though, I don't just think you're beautiful. I think you're the most stunning woman I've ever seen. And I can't wait to be your fake boyfriend tonight."

Shivers spread down my neck where his warm breath tickled over me, and I closed my eyes for a moment, tempted to turn my head and find his lips with mine. But if last night was anything to judge by, letting those primal instincts take over was not a good idea around him. I was at work, and although it was just Bianca, who had become the closest thing I had to a friend, I still wanted to be professional. Damien pulled back, while I tried to steady myself.

He left the trailer, and I watched him go, my breaths coming too fast. Bianca fanned herself dramatically.

"Holy shit, Bree. That was the hot doctor you turned down last night? I would have been all over that like white on rice. You have a willpower I certainly don't possess."

That was just it, though. I was pretty sure I didn't.

9

BREE

Damien insisted on picking me up for our fake/maybe-not-so-fake date that night. Though all that meant was him walking the two steps to my front door and knocking on it. But still. He picked me up and offered me his arm which I took, even though he was being over the top. Truthfully, I was happy for the opportunity to feel his biceps.

We stood side by side in the elevator, my arm pressed against his as we travelled down to the parking garage, and I couldn't help but remember the last time we'd been in here together. Beside me, Damien's breath came out in a forceful hiss, and I had no doubt he was thinking the same thing. But neither of us made a move to pick up where we'd left off last night. I was too damn nervous about seeing my sister for the first time in years. My sister and Tim. The man who'd taken my virginity then tossed me aside for the more experienced model.

Damien drove us in his sleek BMW across the city to a more suburban area. I'd never been over this way, but the houses were new with manicured lawns and parks. It was nice. The sort of area I'd wished I'd grown up in.

We drove in almost total silence, and my nerves got the better of me, street by street. This was going to be a freaking disaster. My sister and I would end up in a screaming match, and my ex or my brother-in-law, whatever the hell he was, would be an asshole. No good was going to come from stirring up old memories like this.

Eventually, Damien pulled the car to a stop. My sister's house was a grey brick home with a shining black door which matched the roof tiles. A gold door knocker sat proudly in the middle, and I tried to imagine myself walking up the neat little path and using it. I couldn't do it.

"We don't have to do this if you don't want to, you know. What do shrinks know anyway? Even us gynos laugh at them. They're bottom of the pecking list at work. Not speaking to your family is no biggie."

I gave him a weak smile. He was trying to make me laugh, and I appreciated it. But laughter wasn't going to get me through this night.

"Do you remember how I told you someone hurt me once?"

He nodded.

"It was them. My sister and her husband. He was my high school sweetheart. He ran off with her, and I didn't hear from either of them again."

He seemed stunned, and it took him a moment to find the words to reply. "That's some seriously shit behaviour on both their behalves." He squinted up at the house. "That really pisses me off actually."

Lights shone in the windows behind closed blinds, and I wondered if they realised we were here.

"So, we're walking into a war zone?"

"I've no idea. Maybe." I forced a laugh. "If it turns into anarchy, I'll understand if you want to bail. There's only so much a fake boyfriend should have to put up with."

"What if he were a real boyfriend?"

I shook my head slowly. "You aren't though, are you?" I didn't give him a chance to answer before I opened the car door and stepped out into the night air. I gulped in a lungful and tried to calm the shaking in my hands. I wasn't sure if it was because of nerves over seeing my sister again, or because things with Damien suddenly felt like they'd stepped up a notch.

Boyfriend? I couldn't do a boyfriend.

I'd only just begun to consider having casual sex with the man. This morning, I'd thought I maybe had some sort of feelings for him, but I hadn't had time to work out what they were. All my relationships sucked and just ended up with me sad and lonely.

I wasn't ready to give Damien up yet. I wasn't ready for him to leave me. So, no. Boyfriend was out of the question. And if I was smart, I'd stick to my celibacy vow and keep him on the line a little longer before giving it all away for free. Enjoy him chasing me.

I didn't want him to be like all the others, but my track record showed that once a guy had slept with me for a while, they lost interest and moved on to shinier, prettier, *nicer* things. I liked the way he looked at me right now and I wanted that to go on as long as possible.

Damien followed me out of the car, his fingers finding mine as we walked up the path to the shiny door. And dammit, a little of my resolve crumbled less than thirty seconds after I'd found it. I was hopeless.

The door opened before I could even knock.

My sister looked exactly the same. It was as if no time had passed. The same shoulder-length brown hair and blue eyes. Long legs, making her the same height as me. She even wore an ankle length dress that was similar to her high school favourite.

"You came. I wasn't sure you would."

I forced a smile, hoping the wobble in my bottom lip wouldn't show. I couldn't cry.

Then a hand on my lower back reminded me I wasn't the only one standing at my sister's front door, and I stepped to the side.

"Sorry. Lou, this is Damien, my ah, boyfriend. Damien, this is my sister, Louise."

Louise turned to greet Damien, but then her eyes widened as she took him in. Something flickered in her gaze, but I couldn't read her anymore and I didn't know what to make of it. She couldn't seriously be checking him out, not while I was standing right here, holding his hand and calling him my boyfriend.

Surely not.

Her gaze scanned over him, and in morbid fascination, with a sinking feeling in my stomach, I turned to face him. His expression was blank.

"Do you two know each other or something?" I asked slowly.

Damien opened his mouth to answer, but Louise cut him off. "No," she said too loudly. Then she lowered her voice. "I mean no. I'm sorry, I just wasn't expecting you to bring a date. You didn't mention you were seeing anyone on the phone." She stuck her hand out in Damien's direction. "It's lovely to meet you, Damien."

I watched the exchange curiously as he took her hand and shook it. "You, too, Louise."

She stepped aside and indicated for us to follow her down the hall, but Damien walked slowly, giving her time to move away before he pulled me to his chest. "You okay? You look like you want to vomit."

"I'm fine." I tried to push him away as we walked into the kitchen area of my sister's house, but he pulled me right back.

"I'm supposed to be your boyfriend, remember?"

Right. That was why he was here. I relaxed my posture and let him drop a kiss onto my bare shoulder. It was such a boyfriend thing to do, and I had to admit, I liked the way it felt. Especially when I realised Tim was watching us from the corner of the room.

I coughed to clear my throat, but the fact that Damien's hand was splayed over my hip did make facing my ex that little bit easier. Tim had put on a few kilos since I'd last seen him, but he was still the man who had broken my teenage heart. And a vindictive part of me wanted him to know what he'd missed out on. I'd dressed to impress, in a skirt with a long slit, showing off my best feature. A feature Tim had always liked. I knew it was catty, but I'd never claimed to be totally reformed.

I was always going to be at least a little part bitch and I wasn't going to apologise for that.

The four of us took our places around the dining room table, and I sat expectantly, waiting for a big, *please forgive us Bree* speech, but it didn't come. Instead, Tim put his arm around Lou as she talked about her job at a local primary school, and how she'd taken up cross fit. Damien quickly joined in, charming as ever, revealing he was also a cross-fitter. Tim let on that he was now a registered nurse, and that sparked a long discussion about medicine and health, which drew me in. Damien, Tim, and I all argued our various specialties with passion, but it broke the tension, and we were all smiling by the end of it. Lou had sat back with satisfaction on her face, as if she'd planed the whole thing.

I got where she was coming from. Somewhere within the discussion, I'd relaxed. Tim and I had banded together to pick on Damien for being a doctor, and the three of us had laughed until our stomachs hurt. I'd forgotten the fact I was sitting in a room with people I hadn't seen in years, and that they'd ever done wrong to me. It was as if the time had slipped away and I suddenly remembered all the late nights Tim, Lou, and I had sat up chatting about school and our friends and just…life. Lou told a story about one of the kids she worked with, and it was as if a light glowed within her. This was the sister I remembered. Happy. Loving. The sister who had cooked dinner with me and helped me with my homework and gossiped about our friends and boys.

By the time we had our roast dinners in front of us, and with Damien's hand on my thigh, I considered that maybe Lou had long realised something I hadn't. Maybe they hadn't apologised because there was so much water under the bridge. Maybe I didn't need an apology from them. I'd thought that was why I'd come here tonight, but it turned out, maybe I'd come to close one door and open another.

I felt nothing when I looked at Tim now. No hint of old feelings remained. Not even the bitterness I'd been carrying around building up in my mind. Seeing them now made me realise that he and I were never meant to be. Although he still looked like the boy I'd dated, he wasn't that boy anymore. He was a man now, with a wife he obviously loved if the adoring glances he kept shooting her were anything to go by. And while any feeling I'd once had for Tim had disappeared, that deep-rooted love for Lou was still there, now springing up from the hard ground as if I'd given it water.

My head was a confusing mess of flip-flopping emotions. This wasn't what I'd expected at all.

Would I ever trust her the way I once had? Probably not, but carrying around all this hurt and resentment towards her was crippling. And I didn't want to be crippled anymore. I wanted to be able to bring a date to her house for a family dinner. Because it turned out, this was kind of nice.

Something else that was nice, was the way Damien's hand was inching up my thigh. How much of this sudden change in my attitude had to do with the man sitting next to me and the maybe feelings I was harbouring for him? We ate our meals, but the minute we'd finished, his fingertips were back on my leg, slipping under the split on my skirt and brushing against my bare skin. A few inches higher and he'd be—

"You're turning pink," he whispered in my ear when Lou and Tim went to get dessert.

"That's because this is supposed to be a fake date, but your hand is travelling to a place that has some not-so-fake needs right now."

He chuckled. "You know, this is your date. I could take care of those not-so-fake needs with a quick trip to the bathroom."

If I wasn't blushing before, the idea of a quickie in the bathroom with him would do it. Images of him leaning me over the bathroom sink, lifting my skirt and him pounding into me from behind made my breath hitch.

"Celibacy vow, remember?" Fucking celibacy vow. I could slap that bitch.

His fingers wandered between my legs, stroking my inner thigh. "If that's what you want…"

I nodded, though if that's what I wanted, why were my legs falling apart, inviting him to move those damn fingers just a few inches north? Damien moved away before Tim and Lou came back into the room, but by then, my skin was on fire and my core ached. I ate my dessert in record time, then stood abruptly, pulling Damien up with me.

"Thank you so much for having us," I said to Lou and Tim. "Damien has an early shift at the hospital tomorrow, and I think we better be going."

"I thought you said you worked at a private—"

"Of course," Lou interrupted her husband with a knowing expression on her face.

Shit. If you were going to make up a lie to end a dinner quickly so you could go make out with your date, you should probably at least make up something plausible. But Lou nodded towards the door and mouthed, *have fun*. A look passed between us, one I remembered well from our younger years. She could still read me like a book. I pulled Damien around the table but stopped in front of her.

"I mean it. Thank you for tonight. I didn't expect to, but I had a nice time."

Lou's eyes turned watery as she pulled me in for a hug. I went stiff, but Lou didn't give up, and after a moment, I relaxed and hugged her back.

"Can we do this again?" she said quietly with a hint of desperation in her voice. "Please? I've missed you."

I nodded and found I meant it. "I'd like that. I'll call you, okay?"

She grinned at me, and I grinned back. I probably should have called to thank Dr Guzman for her good advice. But as Lou closed the door behind us and Damien tilted my head back, claiming my mouth for a long, hot kiss, all I could think about doing was the man whose arms I was standing in.

10

DAMIEN

Bree and I stumbled down the path to my car, and I pressed her up against it, letting her feel exactly how hard up for her I was, while she moaned in my arms and tugged my head down, keeping her lips anchored to mine. Fuck me. She was hot as sin. All long legs and red lips, and all I could think about was getting both of them wrapped around me in one way or another.

Eventually I let her get in the car and practically sprinted around to the driver's side, cursing the fact we'd have to drive the twenty minutes back to the city before I could touch or kiss her again. That was entirely too long.

As soon as I got in the car, Bree was reaching for me across the centre console. Her hand groping my dick made me hiss. "What are you doing?"

"Start the car. Get us home," she demanded.

She didn't need to tell me twice. Within minutes we were back on the main road that led to the city. Bree's fingers popped the button on my jeans before yanking the zipper down and slipping inside my boxer briefs. I groaned as her warm fingers wrapped around my erection and lifted my ass off the seat when she tugged at my pants to give her better access. My cock sprang free, and I concentrated harder on the road. But fuck me. Having my hand up her skirt already tonight had gotten me going, and now, with her hand around my glistening tip, I was in real danger.

"Can you drive if I keep doing this?" she asked, her voice sultry without trying.

Even if I couldn't, I'd pull the damn car over. I wasn't going to ask her to stop.

"Get us home, Damien. Don't stop driving, okay?"

I nodded as her hand moved up and down my shaft. I didn't dare look over at her. I just watched the road and enjoyed the feel of her hand working me over. My eyes rolled back, but I forced myself to concentrate, reaching one hand out to grip her seat.

"Damien."

I twisted my head, and she gave me wicked grin before leaning over and taking my dick into her mouth. My hand immediately dropped to the back of her head and I groaned, long and loud as her hot mouth covered my length. But I kept the pressure light, letting her run this kinky little show. The semi-public blow job was totally getting me off, and as her head bobbed up and down, I knew I wouldn't last the whole way home if she kept that up. But I fought for control the entire way, her tongue circling the head and sucking me deep into her throat.

Fuck me. The woman had some serious blow job skills.

We drove into the darkened parking garage, and when I yanked the hand brake up I knew I wasn't going to last another moment. "Bree," I warned, but she only sucked me harder, and I was done. In an explosion of lust, I pulsed hard and fast into her pretty pink mouth.

I tipped my head against the headrest, not caring if there was anyone else down here, and let my release come. She took everything I had, and when I was done she sat up, her hair messed up from my fingers, her cheeks flushed, her eyes shining. And all I could think of was seeing that look on her face after I'd gotten her naked and made her scream.

"Fuck me, you're so damn sexy." I reached over and found the split in her skirt, running my hand up her thigh as I had at dinner, but this time, I didn't stop. I let my fingers brush the fabric of her underwear. "You're soaked."

She moaned and nodded.

"I'm going to take you upstairs to your apartment and do this right because I'm too damn big to go down on you the way I want to in this tiny car. But I need to taste you now, Bree. I can't wait until we're upstairs. Show me."

With fire in her eyes, her gaze met mine, and she realised what I wanted. She lifted her skirt, revealing the soaking black lace between her legs. She didn't look away when she moved the scrap of fabric aside, revealing her bare pussy to me. Even in the dim light, she glistened.

"Sit back," I commanded, in much the same way as she'd ordered me to drive earlier.

She obeyed, and I ran my hand over her thigh to the centre of her, letting my fingers slip through her wetness to find her clit. She cried out as I touched her, and I knew I could have her coming in minutes, right here in this car. But the anticipation would make it all the better, so instead I rubbed her clit before slipping two fingers inside her. She bucked and threw her head back, but I withdrew my fingers as quickly as I'd inserted them, bringing them to my mouth and licking them clean. I'd meant what I'd said. I just wanted a taste. And now that I'd had it, I was going to take her upstairs and eat her out until she screamed my name.

Was oral sex really breaking a celibacy vow? I was pretty sure it didn't count.

BREE

Damien had barely touched me, and I was already on the verge of orgasm. Sucking him off while he drove had me wet and ready, and then him demanding to see me… He'd pretty much done me in right then, right there. But then he was pulling me from the car and tugging me towards the elevator, ramming his finger repetitively over the up button, though we both knew it would only come when it wanted.

I was as antsy as he was, sex on the brain and the taste of him still on my tongue. I bounced on the balls of my feet, desperate to get more of him inside me than just his fingers. "Stairs," I decided, too impatient to wait for the decrepit elevator.

Yanking my heels off, I led him to the stairwell next to the elevator shaft. I lifted my skirt so I didn't trip on it, then the two of us raced the four flights of stairs, bursting into our hallway with a laugh. We stumbled towards my apartment, stopping to make out twice along the way.

We eventually made it inside, and he kicked the door closed behind him. We stared at each other in the dim light, but neither of us made a move to towards the switch. Instead he came to me, tilting my chin up and capturing my lips with his. His mouth was softer this time, the urgency of his kisses in the hallway replaced with something quieter. I moaned into his mouth his tongue stroking against mine, firing up my entire body once more. His hands skimmed down my sides, running over each curve before he found the hem of my top and lifted it over my head. My bra came off next, and he swooped down to suck my nipple, his fingers hooking in the waistband of my skirt, sliding it down my legs along with my underwear. I stood completely bare, while he was still fully dressed. He stepped back and let his gaze travel me from head to toe, then he shook his head and swore. He dug his fingers into my hips, lifting me to the kitchen table and covering my body with his. He pushed me back so I was lying spread across the table like a meal. Damien's lips travelled down my body, heading for the spot I wanted him most. His tongue rasped over my skin as he knelt, slinging my legs over his shoulders and opening me to him fully.

Without a pause, he licked right through the centre of me, and I grasped the edges of the table for fear of bucking right off it. "You're already close, aren't you? I can tell," he murmured, and I nodded uselessly.

He inserted two fingers and covered my clit with wet heat, and I ground on him, angling my body the way I needed to and urging him to go faster, rocking against his hand and mouth. And he didn't disappoint. He moved back, circling my clit with his thumb before pressing on it, and I was done.

"Damien!" I cried as I spasmed around his fingers and reached down to clutch at his hair, but he didn't stop. He worked me until I was a boneless heap, bare and sated on my kitchen table. I wondered how I'd ever eat there again. But who cared.

His chuckle rumbled around the room and his face appeared above mine. "I'm not done with you yet," he warned, but to my ears, it sounded more like a promise.

He gathered me in his arms and walked us into my bedroom, while I took the opportunity to kiss his neck and earlobe. He pulled the covers back before he put me down, and then I watched the show as he undid the buttons on his shirt and pushed down his pants that were still open from our exploits in the car. I took in the tattoos that not only covered his arm and chest but dipped low, close to where his cock was already hard again, and continued down his leg. He climbed into bed with me, and within moments we were tangled up together. And the feel of his bare skin against mine was almost more mind-blowing that the orgasm I'd just had on the kitchen table. He laid on top of me, supporting himself on his forearms, his cock pressing into my leg. With an open mouth, he kissed a path up and down my neck until he found my lips.

Damien kissed me long and deep and slow. And we stayed like that for a long time. Just lying together, enjoying the feel of a warm body. But before long, an ache opened up inside me again, and squirmed beneath him, opening my legs and rubbing against him to try to find relief. His hand travelled to my breast, cupping it and fondling the already hard nipple, and it did nothing to quell the desire that throbbed between my legs.

"Damien. Please. I need you. Inside me."

"Your vow. No sex, remember?"

What? As if I cared about the stupid vow! "If you don't fuck me right now I'm going to implode."

He moved back and looked me in the eye, then searched my face to see if I meant it. I did. Eleven months and one week was enough.

"I'm serious. I want you."

He licked a trail along my neck to my ear. "You sure?"

He shifted so his cock pressed my entrance, and my eyes rolled back in my head, but I managed to moan my approval. Then he was off the bed and producing his wallet from the pocket of the pants that lay in a heap on the floor. He pulled out a condom, rolled it over his length, and was back on top of me in seconds, nudging my legs apart.

"Don't be gentle."

He grinned. "Thank fuck you said that because I'm not sure I could be, even if I wanted to." And with that, he pushed inside me with one long, hard thrust.

I saw stars.

True to his word, he fucked me hard and deep, lifting one of my legs up over his shoulder until we were both teetering on the edge.

"Don't stop," I whispered.

He dropped his mouth and kissed me, his hips slamming against mine, the bedframe hitting the wall. Pleasure coiled low and deep before unleashing through me in a way I'd never felt before, and I fell apart in his arms, his lips silencing my cries.

Then his big body shuddered over mine, finding his own release. He buried his face in my neck, and I dug my fingernails into his back while we pulsed together. I lowered my leg to wrap around his waist and he let his weight rest on top of me, both of us slick with sweat, breathing hard.

Eventually, he sweetly kissed my neck and rolled to his side. He held his arm out to me, and I snuggled into his chest, surprised at how much I liked the feel of his arms around me. I'd never been much of a snuggler, but lying with my head on Damien's chest, tracing his tattoos with my fingertips, sated and happy from the marathon sex session we'd just had was the most content and relaxed I'd felt in ages. I wasn't actively fighting to be calm either. I wasn't using yoga breathing or anger management techniques. I just…was.

My stomach growled, and Damien lifted his head. "Hungry much?"

"I kind of am." I sat up and leant over the side of the bed to where I'd left my laptop yesterday. When I straightened, Damien gaze was all over my bare skin. I shook my head. "Perv. I'm going to order some Uber Eats. You want something?"

His eyes darkened, and his lips made a beeline for my breast. "Yes, but not food."

I laughed, pushing him away. "Food first." The laptop flickered on, and as usual the internet connection was out. I choked on a laugh when I brought up the network connection page.

"What?" Damien asked curiously, looking over my shoulder, then burst into laughter.

There, in the list of available networks, right where Damien's House of Debauchery once was, was a network called Take it easy on that bed! My face went pink at the thought of his roommates hearing every groan and moan we'd made for the past few hours.

But Damien just turned around and thumped on the wall connecting his apartment with mine. "You're one to talk, Jess!"

Jess' and Millie's laughter was as clear as if we'd been in the same room.

1 2

BREE

amien didn't leave my bed until almost lunchtime on Sunday. We'd stuffed ourselves on Chinese takeaway in the middle of the night and slept for a few hours before I'd woken up with his erection pressing against my lower back. No point in wasting good morning wood, I'd climbed on top of him and woken him up in the best way possible.

We'd showered together, and eventually I'd had to kick him out because I needed to study. But little butterflies flittered around my belly at how content he'd seemed to hang around. And I liked having him there.

I'd pulled my books out and tried to concentrate on my notes, but my mind kept straying. Damien's touch still lingered on my skin, and every time I closed my eyes, all I saw was him. It was making me giddy with excitement. Like a teenager with a crush, but I didn't even care. I did have a crush on him. A pretty huge one. One that perhaps had strings attached. Strings I feared might have been attached to my heart.

I needed to snap out of it. It was times like this that I wished I had a girlfriend. Someone I could ring and spill all the dirty hot details to and analyse what the whole thing meant. I had Bianca, but although we talked each day at work, we weren't really in the habit of chatting outside of it.

I wanted to call my sister. We'd gotten along so well last night, and for years she'd been my go-to person. And even though we'd fallen out, that desire to run to her when things went wrong, or when things were great, had never gone away. I'd missed her to my very core. Seeing her had made me miss her all the more. And this morning, for the first time in so long, I was happy. Maybe Lou and I would never be what we once were, but last night had shown me that time had certainly healed some old wounds.

I picked up my phone, found her number in my saved contacts, and hit the little green button. She picked up on the first ring.

"Hey, Lou…" I said as I stood and walked to my bedroom with my phone. I plonked down on the mattress, the springs squeaking, reminding me of the last time they'd done that. I tried not to giggle. "It's Bree," I added lamely.

"I know, you goose. There's this thing called caller ID. Why do you sound like you're smiling?"

I grinned. "Because I am."

"Does that have anything to do with the hot doctor you brought to my house last night?"

"Maybe."

"You had hot monkey sex all night, didn't you?"

I burst out laughing. "Yes. But it's not just the sex. Though that was mind-blowing. I like him, Lou. He's sweet, and funny, and thoughtful."

"And sexy."

And just like that, we were back to normal. "Super sexy."

"So, what's the problem?"

"The problem is, I don't know if he feels the same. I might just be a one-night stand. And I don't think I want to be."

She paused. "What do you mean? Aren't you two together? You looked pretty together last night."

I bit my lip. Shit. I was the worst liar ever. "We…I…kind of lied last night. He's not my boyfriend. Truth is, I only met him last week." I winced. It sounded bad when I laid it all out like that. "We just pretended to be a couple last night because I didn't want to face you and Tim and feel like the loser little sister again."

She let out a long sigh. "Oh, Bree. You never were. We were the ones who messed up. I wanted to tell you last night how sorry we were, but then everything was going well, and I didn't want to ruin it. You deserve so much more than an apology, and I know I'll have to work hard to regain your trust. But I really want to. I'm so sorry, Bree. I have been every day since it happened."

Tears flooded my eyes. I might not have needed the apology like I thought I had, but it was still nice to have. "Thank you. And I'm sorry about lying."

Lou made a dismissive sound.

"So, what do I do about Damien?"

"Well, the two of you had me completely fooled. I thought you were completely in love. Maybe you were acting, but I doubt either of you are that good. Maybe your acting skills were enhanced by real feelings? And I'd say they aren't just on your side. Maybe you didn't notice the way his eyes followed you around the room. Or the way he was constantly finding reasons to touch you. But I noticed. And it made me happy you'd found someone who cared so much about you."

I flopped back on my bed. "I don't know. He said he's a relationship sort of guy, but look at him. He's a young, hot doctor. And he fucks like he's had plenty of practice." I didn't know what to think. I wanted last night to have been real.

And Lou was wrong. I had noticed the way he'd touched me and the way his gaze had followed me. I'd noticed, because I noticed everything about him. I'd been hard pressed to keep focussed on the dinner conversation, when every part of me felt drawn in Damien's direction. When every touch was so distracting, I'd barely been able to keep myself out of his lap.

"He's not like that," Lou said.

"You only met him last night." Then I frowned, remembering the way she'd looked at Damien when she'd first opened the door. "Didn't you?"

"You're letting your hang-ups from what Tim and I did cloud your judgement. If he says he's a relationship sort of guy, believe him. Has he given you a reason to think otherwise?"

"No."

"Then give the guy the benefit of the doubt. Not everyone in your life will cheat and lie." Her voice cracked.

"Lou…"

"No, don't smooth this over. It's true. I deserve it."

"We were kids. And we're talking again now. Things can only go up from here, okay?'

She let out a shaky breath. "Just please don't let what we did ruin your chances at happiness. I couldn't bear it."

I didn't think I could either. But with my sister back in my life and something maybe starting up with Damien, my happiness in that moment was hard to put a damper on.

13

DAMIEN

I couldn't stop thinking about Bree's damn long legs. Her delicate ankles and shapely calves. And the smooth skin that led to thighs I could lay between all day and never get bored. That skirt she'd worn on Saturday night, with a thigh-high split had been my undoing. I'd known from the minute she'd stepped out into the hall that I was a goner. There was no way I was going to be able to keep my hands to myself for the entire night. And thank god, I hadn't had to. The blow job she'd given me in the car had replayed in my mind all day as I'd followed up on a pile of overdue paperwork. Her crimson lips wrapped around my cock as we'd driven through the city streets…the way she'd not even flinched when I'd come, then demanded more. Fuck.

Cleo stuck her head through my office doorway, startling me. "You okay?"

I straightened in my seat and focussed on her. "Of course."

"You know it's five-thirty? Time for you to quit day dreaming about your sexual conquests and go home. Everyone else has already left, I think."

I shook my head. I'd swear the woman was a mind reader. She

always knew what I was thinking. Which made her an ideal assistant. But there was no keeping secrets from her. She was too damn perceptive.

A door slammed from the front of the clinic, and Cleo sighed, looking into the hall. "Not as alone as I thought we were. I'll get rid of them. We officially closed a few minutes ago."

I nodded and packed up my things, trying to come up with some sort of pun or gimmick I could use to lure Bree over to my place tonight. I'd done the pizza and the coffee thing, and she'd seemed to think it was funny. I liked making her laugh.

"Please. I just need to see him for a moment," a woman's voice pleaded from the reception area.

"I'm sorry, he's finished for the day. I can make you an emergency appointment for tomorrow if you like? Mrs Braun, isn't it?"

I scrambled to my feet and rushed into the hallway where Lou stood with Cleo. "It's fine. I'll see her."

Cleo gave me an exasperated look behind Lou's back and glared at the clock on the wall.

"Just leave the front door open. I'll lock up when we're done."

She shrugged but grabbed her handbag from her desk, and with a wave over her shoulder, she left. I turned back to Lou.

"Hi, again."

"I'm so sorry to barge in like this. I came straight from work. Can we talk?"

"Of course. Do you want to come sit in my office? We're alone, so we can talk here, but my office is more comfortable."

She nodded, and I ushered her out of the reception area. She sat gingerly on the edge of the chair opposite my desk.

"I can't be your patient anymore," she said in a rush. "I'm so sorry, if I'd known you were dating my sister I would have never come here in the first place. I really hope you didn't feel too awkward on Saturday night."

She twisted her hands on her lap.

"Not at all. I was surprised to see you, of course. And I totally understand why you need to change doctors."

"It's nothing personal. I just can't have my sister's boyfriend looking at my vagina then face him over Sunday night dinner."

I choked out a laugh. "Understandable." I liked the idea of Sunday night dinner with Bree's family. I was an only child, and my parents lived out of state. Family dinners were a foreign concept to me, but they sounded nice. "Just let reception know which doctor you'll be transferring to and I'll have them send over your files. But while you're here, your test results should be in. Do you want me to go through them with you, or would you prefer to do that with your new doctor?"

She bit her lip. "Would you mind? I know it's after hours, but I've been nervous all week about the results. I don't know when I'll be able to get an appointment with someone else."

"No problem." I turned my monitor back on and brought up her file, quickly scanning through the results of the tests I'd sent her for. My heart sank with every line I read. I cleared my throat as I stood to walk around the desk and sit in the chair next to her.

"It's not good, is it?" she whispered.

Most of the time, I loved my job. I loved helping people. But this was the side I hated. I hated having to ruin someone's dreams.

"No. It's not. Did you know you have endometriosis?"

She shook her head.

"It would be the cause of your painful periods. I'm going to recommend your new doctor do a laparoscopy and check it out more thoroughly."

"But you think that's why I haven't fallen pregnant?"

I nodded. "Most likely. The ultrasound you had shows quite a severe case." I took her hand, even though it was unprofessional. But I'd had dinner with the woman over the weekend, and she felt more like a friend than a patient. And she wouldn't be my patient after this conversation was finished anyway.

"But I'll still be able to have children? It can be fixed? With surgery or medication?"

I squeezed her hand. "Your doctor will be able to tell you more after the surgery."

She squeezed her eyes shut. "Don't do that. Just tell me."

I sighed. "I really don't know. Your scans show a severe case. Just from looking at them, I'd highly doubt you'll be able to fall pregnant naturally. IVF may be an option."

Her face crumpled. "May?"

"I just can't say for sure, without actually getting in there and having a look. I'm so sorry, Lou. I know this isn't the news you were hoping for."

She stood, and I did too, still holding her hand.

She took a deep breath, but her fingers shook, and a sob burst from her chest. "I just don't know what I'm going to tell Tim. He wants a baby so badly. So do I. We've been trying so long."

A tear slipped down her cheek, and it broke my damn heart. Her scans were bad. I'd tried to sugarcoat it as much as possible, but I highly doubted a laparoscopy was going to yield good results. If anything, I suspected it might actually be worse. Lou's shoulders shook as her head dropped, and my gut twisted. She knew. She knew exactly what I wasn't saying. I pulled her into my arms and let her cry on my chest. Her arms were limp at her sides, but I felt her misery in every sob.

Eventually, she quieted and looked up at me. "I'm sorry, I—"

"What the hell?" a shrill voice came from the doorway.

My head snapped up and I dropped my arms, jumping away from around Lou. Bree stood in the doorway, those red lips I'd been dreaming of all day pressed into a snarl. Her long legs were bare, black stilettos on her feet, and damn. A trench coat tied at her waist. My mouth dried. She had to be naked underneath.

It would have been hot as hell, and I would have thrown her across my desk and gone to town on her. If she hadn't just caught me with another woman in my arms.

"Bree," I started, but her gaze swung from me to Lou, her eyes widening when she recognised her sister. Then filled with tears.

"No," she said, backing out of the room. "I'm not doing this. Not again."

I opened my mouth to tell her why I was hugging her sister, but doctor-patient confidentiality prevented me from actually saying the words. Shit! I couldn't tell her Lou was here as my patient. I'd be breaking an oath I believed in. Even though I wanted to tell her everything, it wasn't my place. "Bree," I pleaded, and she fixed me to the spot with fire in her eyes. I abruptly shut my mouth. She seemed mad enough to cut my dick off, and I wasn't sure if there were scissors on my desk.

Lou rushed forward, her hands outstretched. "Wait! Bree, this isn't what it looks like!"

"Oh, isn't it?" she snarled, her face distorted with anger. "It looks exactly like how I found you and Tim. And those were the exact same words you used back then, too." She shook her head. "No. I'm not doing this again. The two of you and Tim can all do whatever the hell you want. You deserve each other."

She spun on her heel, and a moment later the front door slammed.

"Excuse me, but what on earth is all the yelling about?"

Lou and I both turned to the male voice behind us, and my heart sank. "Dr Simpson. I didn't realise you were still here."

"Well, I am."

So he was. The CEO of the whole damn company. Witnessing two upset women yelling at me.

"Care to explain yourself?"

I may as well have lit my promotion on fire.

Lou glanced at me in panic. "I'm going after her. I'm so sorry. This was inappropriate."

I cringed at the use of the word inappropriate and the concerned furrowing of Dr Simpson's forehead. I was going to be dragged over the coals by HR for this, I could just see it. Lou grabbed her bag and cardigan from the floor and ran for the door.

I ran after her, not caring that Dr Simpson was still waiting for an explanation, and grabbed her arm, spinning her around. "Stop, Lou!"

"What are you doing? Didn't you see her face? I've got to go after her."

I shook my head. "No. I do. Please. Let me."

14

BREE

The door slammed shut so hard the walls of my entire apartment shook. Un-fucking-believable! Damien and I hadn't made any commitments to each other, but the man had spent all weekend in my bed, and now, less than twenty-four hours later, he was standing in an embrace with another woman. And not just any woman. My sister.

It was my own stupid fault. I'd seen the look on Lou's face when we'd arrived at her house, and I'd ignored it. She either knew him, or she'd been checking him out. I wasn't sure which, but it didn't matter. The end result was still the same. I don't know why I'd thought things were any different. Once a cheater, always a cheater.

A little voice in the back of my head said that wasn't fair. I'd cheated once, too, and hadn't I reformed myself? But when slapped in the face with the evidence, as I'd just been, there wasn't much option other than to admit the truth.

My initial assessment of Damien as a manwhore was obviously correct. Were we some sort of conquest to him? Find a set of sisters to sleep with and tick it off your bucket list? Bile rose in my throat. He was disgusting. My cheeks burned with embarrassment, and I pulled off my heels and threw them into my wardrobe so hard one bounced back out. What had I been thinking? Rocking up at his work in a damn trench coat? Stupid, Bree. Stupid. I tried to slow my out-of-control breathing, but it was no use, I was too worked up. I had so much adrenaline coursing through me I could go a round with Mike Tyson. Or preferably, Damien. I'd get a sick sort of enjoyment in cracking his perfectly straight nose. Asshole.

Thumping from the front door echoed around my quiet apartment. "Bree!"

Speaking of assholes, one was at my door.

More thumping. "Bree! Open the damn door, or I swear to god, I'll kick it down."

I rolled my eyes. And people thought I was dramatic. I stomped across the apartment and yanked open the door. "What!"

Damien's gaze darkened when his eyes met mine, and he stormed into the apartment, giving me no choice but to scuttle backwards or be mowed down. The door slammed shut behind him.

"What the fuck was all that about?" he yelled. He shoulders heaved, and he was breathing as fast as I was.

"I was about to ask you the same thing! How do you know Lou? Were you already sleeping with her when we hooked up? Is this some sort of game to you? I knew the two of you recognised each other at dinner, but neither of you said anything so I thought I was just being paranoid. Letting old fears cloud my judgement, but I should have trusted my gut instinct. What the hell is wrong with the two of you? You're both sick!" The firey words flew from my mouth.

"What the hell is wrong with me? What's wrong with you?! I'm not sleeping with your goddamn sister! And I'm not this playboy you seem to think I am! I already told you, I'm a relationship sort of guy. I've never had a goddamn one-night stand in my life." The anger in his gaze suddenly changed, morphing into something slow and hot as it travelled over my body. "And I don't plan for you to be my first."

Despite my anger, my damn traitorous body glowed under his attention.

"Take off that coat, Bree."

I froze. "What? No! Didn't you hear what I—"

"I heard. And I also told you that your arguments are complete bullshit. There is nothing going on with your sister. Now take it off."

He stalked towards me, like a lion ready to devour me, and damn if it wasn't the hottest thing I'd ever seen. I'd only seen a tiny glimpse of this dominant, alpha side of him, but it was thrilling, if not a little shocking, to be in the direct path of it. The idea of him bossing me around in bed was hot as fuck, and my core throbbed at the thought of having him rip off my clothes. I held up a hand in a stop motion before he could touch me. He stopped immediately.

"I just want you to know, we're not done with this argument." But I unbuckled the belt from around my waist, slowly, watching his eyes flare.

"You want to fight some more? Fine." He gritted out the words like they were causing him physical pain.

His fingers clenched at his sides when I let the front of the coat open, revealing my nudity to him. He groaned, and I wished I still had the heels on. The coat slipped down my arms, pooling on the floor at my feet, and I closed the space between our bodies. His breath came in rapid bursts, and the muscles in his shoulders tensed with the strain of holding himself back. I'd told him to stop, and he was respecting that, waiting for some sort of signal from me, letting me know the ball was still in my court.

I untucked his shirt from his pants and pushed it up his torso until he pulled it off. He trembled slightly when I let my fingers trail over his chest and abs, down to the trail of dark hair that led into his tailored work pants. Brazen, I flipped the button and ran my hand down into his boxer briefs, palming his hard length. A hiss sounded from between his teeth and his resolve broke. He grabbed my wrist with one hand as the other fisted the back of my hair, yanking it back so I was forced to look at him. The tingling in my scalp only turned me on more.

"You don't run this show, Bree. Not tonight."

I whimpered. Fucking whimpered! Who was I right now? A puddle at his feet, that's what I was. And I liked it. He roughly spun me around and slammed his chest against my back. His lips found my neck. He kissed and sucked his way down to my shoulders, nipping at the skin with his teeth. Each tiny sting, then smoothed over with his tongue. My legs parted as if they had a mind of their own, and his thick cock slid through the wetness there, searching for my entrance.

I leant into the wall in front of me, using it for support as his fingers found my clit, making me cry out. I pushed back into him, aching to be filled.

"Still want to fight? Cos I can fuck that desire right out of you."

I'd already forgotten what we were fighting about, and I wanted nothing more than for him to fuck me senseless. His cock ran through my folds again, and I moaned when his fingers worked my most sensitive spot.

"I'm on the pill," I whispered, desperate to have him inside me.

He stilled against my back. "I've never done it without a condom."

"Me neither."

The head of his cock slipped inside me, and we both groaned.

"You sure?" His words were husky, and I slammed my hips back, engulfing his entire length in answer. My fingernails pressed into the plasterboard and I arched my back, taking everything he had to give.

Damien pounded into me, one hand gripping my hip, the

other alternating between my clit and my nipples as he leant over me, working until a spiral of pleasure built within me. He moved in practiced rhythm, and then the pressure became too much and I cried out my release. I twisted my head as far back as I could, and he met my lips with his, devouring me with his kiss, his tongue invading my mouth while his dick filled my core. He thrust into me, with long, hard strokes until I was a mewling mess, then with a final thrust, he yelled out coming inside of me, my body still clenching around him.

My legs wobbled, but his arm tightened around my waist and he buried his face into my neck.

"I had no idea it could be like that," he murmured.

With every nerve ending in my body still tingling, I agreed.

Afterwards, we showered together, and I ran my soapy fingers over his chest and down his abs before shoving him to the bathroom floor and riding him again, unable to get enough of him. When we were finally done, we fell into bed in a tangle of arms and legs, and he pulled me on top of him. He propped his hands behind his head, and I kissed the light dusting of dark hair on his chest before resting my chin there so we were looking at each other.

"You know nothing is going on between your sister and I, don't you?"

I nodded sheepishly. "I believe you. I'm sorry I was such a psycho in your office. I have some impulse control issues, if you hadn't noticed. I tend to fly off the handle."

He chuckled and pushed a lock of damp hair out of my eye. "I noticed. But I like you anyway."

"I like you, too," I whispered. Which was exactly why I'd gotten so crazy in the first place. Somewhere our fake relationship had turned into something real. Something I didn't want to lose. The idea of losing it had sent me completely postal.

A thought occurred to me and filled me with horror. "Is my

outburst today going to cost you your promotion? Shit, Damien! I'm so sorry."

He grimaced. "I'll sort it out. I'll just tell the bosses that you're one of my patients and full of fertility drugs. They tend to make people a little crazy."

I laughed and slapped him across the chest. "You're such a shit."

He shrugged. "Never claimed to be a saint."

He may not have been a saint, but he was a nice guy. But I still needed to know…

"Why was my sister at your office today?"

"You know I can't tell you that."

Something clicked in my head. "She's your patient?" The thought hadn't even occurred to me when I'd seen her in his arms.

He gave me an exasperated look.

"Right. I'll ask my sister."

"Good. I'm glad we got that out of the way. Because I don't really want to be talking about your sister while you're lying naked on top of me."

I sniggered. "No?" I wriggled, his cock thickening beneath me.

He flipped me on my back and dropped his lips to mine for a hot, lingering kiss. "No, Bree. Talking is the last thing I want to do right now."

BREE

$\mathcal{I}$ shifted my weight from foot to foot as I waited on Lou and Tim's doorstep.

The door swung open, and Lou's face appeared, a mixture of surprise and relief. "Bree!"

She stepped forward, raising her hands, and for a moment, I thought she was going to hug me. But then she obviously thought better of it and dropped them like a dead weight.

"I'm really glad you came. I've been trying to call you. Did Damien talk to you?"

I nodded. "Can I come in?"

She stepped aside, and I led the way to the kitchen we'd eaten dinner in a few nights before. Tim was sitting at the table, but when he lifted his head and saw it was me, his eyes darted straight to where Lou stood. I don't know what sort of look she gave him, but he offered a tight smile and hightailed it for the safety of the living room.

We took seats across from each other, and Lou opened her mouth to speak, but I cut her off. "Wait. Please. Let me go first. I really stuffed up yesterday at Damien's office. I just… I jumped to conclusions. Damien told me nothing is going on. You know, romantically, between the two of you."

Lou shook her head rapidly and grabbed my hands from across the table. "There's not. I swear. I know I haven't earned back your trust yet, but I swear. Things are different now. I was a stupid teenager when Tim and I …well. You know what we did. I didn't realise what I'd be throwing away.

"I did recognise Damien, when you brought him here on Saturday night." She cast a glance over her shoulder at Tim in the living room, but he was engrossed in a football game and not paying us any attention. "Damien is my fertility doctor. Was. I went in yesterday to see him and to tell him I needed to change doctors, because now he's dating you, it would be a conflict of interest." She gave me a wry grin. "And also super awkward for my sister's boyfriend to be, you know, down there."

I choked on a laugh. There was that.

She sobered. "He agreed, but he'd already done some tests, and he had the results. They weren't good. And I was upset. He was just being a nice guy, Bree. I swear. There was nothing more to that embrace than him letting a patient cry on his shoulder."

I squeezed her fingers. "I didn't realise you guys were trying. You're so young still to have fertility problems. It never even crossed my mind. What's going to happen now? You'll find another doctor?"

She bit her lip. "Yes. Damien referred me to a friend of his. He said I'll have to have a small surgery, so they can get in there and really have a proper poke around. And that will determine where we go from here. Maybe it'll be IVF. Maybe we'll foster or adopt." She looked past me to where Tim sat. "We'll make it happen, one way or the other. Tim is meant to be a dad. He'd be great at it."

"And you'll be great at being a mother, too. You practically raised me."

She nodded. "Let me give you some motherly advice then.

Don't wait to have babies. Find the right guy, then make me an aunty."

I sat back in my chair. "Settle. I'm not even thinking about babies yet." I wasn't even sure I wanted any. Lou had always been the mothering type, but I wasn't sure I had any maternal instincts.

She laughed. "I don't know. Maybe you'll be thinking about it sooner than you think. What's happening with Damien?"

"I like him," I admitted. "I like him a lot."

"He's a nice guy." She smiled fondly at the back of her husband's head. "The good guys are few and far between. So when you find one, you should hang on to him."

She looked back and gave me a wink. "Lock it down, little sister."

16

DAMIEN

TWO WEEKS LATER...

*T*oo impatient to wait for the elevator, I bounded up the stairs of my apartment building two at a time and sprinted down the hallway to Bree's door. We'd spent every day for the last few weeks together, and I always came home straight to her apartment. I'd really only left it to get fresh clothes and go to work. The rest of the time we'd been holed up in our own little love nest. Normally I just let myself in, but today I slid to a stop as the deafening wailing from inside caught my attention. What the fuck?

I knocked, but nothing happened so I tried the doorknob. It twisted in my hand, and I poked my head around the corner. "Bree?"

She looked up and grinned from behind a microphone, then turned back to finish belting out the song she was massacring. Jess and Millie sat on her lounge. Millie had a glass of wine in her hand and sang along with Bree, while Jess painted her nails.

"Hey, stranger! We haven't seen you in weeks!" Jess cried when she noticed me.

I looked from woman to woman, with no idea what I'd just stumbled upon. There were already two empty wine bottles on the coffee table in front of them. "Does someone want to explain why you're all home from work, day drinking and murdering a Bryan Adams song?" I'd liked that song, before I'd entered this room. I wasn't sure I'd ever be able to unhear Bree's rendition, though.

The world's worst duo ignored me and kept up their butchering, but Jess turned to answer my question. "Millie and I played hooky from work. And Bree had an early call time, so she was home. What else is there to do on a Friday afternoon? We knew you'd come straight here after work."

I undid the top button on my shirt and dumped my stuff on Bree's kitchen table before I walked over to her and pushed the microphone away from her mouth. "Hey, rockstar."

She grinned and stretched up on her toes to kiss me. Her mouth tasted sweet from the wine, and I pulled her close as her lips parted. Her eyes were glassy when we broke apart, and she gave me a huge grin. "You're here just in time!"

I tugged her over to the single armchair and sat her down onto my lap. "In time for what?"

"We were just about to play Truth or Dare!" Millie announced, pouring me a glass of wine and handing it across the table.

"What are we, twelve?" I took a sip, and it was sweet as sugar. Not what I'd normally drink, but alcohol was alcohol. And on a Friday afternoon, I wasn't too concerned with what I drank.

"You can go first for that smart-assery then, Damo," Millie declared, shooting me a filthy look. "Truth or Dare?"

"Truth. But go easy on me, because you're all tipsy, and I'm very sober."

"Fine. I'll save the juicy ones for when you're drunk and more willing to spill your guts. Why are you home from work before five anyway?"

"Is that your question? I'm home because I got the promotion, and the boss said I could leave early to celebrate."

Bree twisted to look at me. "You did?"

I nodded. Then all three women were on top of me, yelling their congratulations and slapping me on the back and messing my hair up. I laughed and pushed Jess and Millie off, who sank back into their seats with a laugh.

"I'm so relieved," Bree spoke against my ear.

I knew she still felt bad about the scene she'd created in my office, but as I'd told her, I'd smoothed it over with a little white lie, and evidently, nobody had held it against me.

"Your turn, Millie."

"What? No, you haven't had your turn! That wasn't a truth or dare question!"

"Was."

"Nope."

Jess rolled her eyes. "Don't start, you two."

Millie and I could go on ribbing each other like children for days, but it was all in good fun. I winked at Millie, and she laughed.

"I don't think that was a proper turn either. And actually, I have one for you," Bree said quietly. She had been smiling and laughing but now she suddenly looked serious.

My mouth dried because something gave me the impression this question wasn't going to be as easy as why I was home from work early.

"Okay, shoot," I agreed, while Millie mumbled something about playing favourites.

Bree shifted on my lap so we were face to face. "What are we? Are we a couple? Are we just friends that hook up? I'm falling for you and I don't want to fall on my face."

From the corner of my eye, I saw Millie's mouth drop open.

"Oh wow, look at that. Time for us to leave!" Jess yelled, picking up the half-empty wine bottle with one hand and pulling Millie off the lounge with the other.

"What? No, I want to hear what he says!" Millie whined. Then she glared at me. "You'd better answer this one correctly, Damo. Or it won't just be Bree who's out for your balls. We like this one."

I shook my head as Jess dragged her out of the front door.

I turned back to Bree who hadn't cracked a smile.

"Sorry. That probably wasn't the best time to ask you, but I've been trying to ask you all week."

"You have?"

She nodded. "I'm sorry. I know I'm putting you on the spot, but I just need to know. I don't want this to be casual. I like you. A lot. A whole lot more than I ever thought possible, especially considering we met when you mowed me down on your bike and gave me a concussion."

"So wasn't a concussion," I chuckled.

"We joke around, but I'm serious. I want this. Do you?" She twisted her hands on her lap.

I grasped her chin between my fingers, angling her head so she couldn't look down. "I've wanted this from the moment I knocked you off your bike, Bree. Truth is, it wasn't just the phone call that had me distracted that day. When I saw you lying there on the ground, all beat up and bruised and swearing at me, all I could think was you were the sexiest woman I'd ever seen."

"You have some serious issues, you know that, right?"

"I know. But you were, and you are. And now you're so much more than just a pretty face. You're smart, committed, and driven. And you're a wild cat in bed..."

She elbowed me in the chest, and I grunted but found her fingers and threaded mine between them. I'd held her hand dozens of times over the past few weeks now, and each time it was a comforting gesture. Her hand fit in mine like it had been specifically crafted to do so. "I like being around you, Bree. You bring out sides of me I didn't even know existed." She blushed, and I wondered if she was thinking about the sex we'd had in every room and in every position all over this apartment. She let me boss her around in bed, and I let her boss me around outside of it. We worked. "You were mine from the minute I met you. You didn't know it, and maybe I didn't either, but we were always going to end up here. I should have said it out loud before this, but as far as I'm concerned, we've been a couple this entire time. And I intend to be a couple for a whole lot longer. Because the truth is, I'm not just falling for you. I've fallen for you." I trailed the back of my fingers down her soft cheek. "I think I'm in love with you, Bree.

"You think?" she whispered.

I shook my head, trying to smother my grin. "No. I just said that because I didn't want to scare you. I love you. I do. I have for a while now."

That smile of hers nearly bowled me over.

"You love me."

"Yep."

The grin reached her eyes, and they sparkled like fucking diamonds, stealing my breath. She was stunning. And she was mine. I didn't need her to say it back if she wasn't ready. This thing between us was so damn right, and I was so confident in it that I knew without a doubt she'd get there in her own time. I pulled her head down so her lips met mine and I kissed her like I'd never kissed her before. She moulded her mouth to mine, and I ran my tongue along her lips, pushing my way inside her mouth, finding her tongue with mine and loving the little moans she made as I stole *her* breath.

She eventually pulled away, pressing her forehead to mine. "I love you, too. I was so scared of my feelings. I didn't even want to admit them to myself. This thing between us? It's right, isn't it? I know it started off as a fake relationship, but it never really felt that way to me. I can't believe we're here just a few weeks later saying I love you. I would have never picked this in a million years."

She laughed, and the happy noise echoed around the room, filling my heart. I wanted to see that look of pure happiness every day. And if she'd let me, I'd do my best to always keep it that way.

"We're not fake, Bree. We never have been. And that's the truth."

THE END

Want a free Only You book? Only the Lies is Cleo's story and it's free when you join my reader family newsletter! It's free to join here!

MISSING Reese and Low from Only the Positive? Need an update on them? Pick up the next book in the Only You series.

Only the Negatives is Reese's sister Gemma's story. She's all grown up and a strong, sassy, paraplegic woman. Watch her get her HEA here! As well as updates on your old friends, Jamison and Elodie, and Bianca and Riley! Or keep reading for a sneak peek!

ONLY YOU
#3
ONLY THE
NEGATIVES
ELLE THORPE

CHAPTER 1

GEMMA

The open sores on my hands left a trail of bright red blood as I dabbed them gingerly on my jeans and cursed myself for not grabbing my gloves. A rookie mistake I hadn't made in years. But I also hadn't expected to have to push myself thirty kilometres along broken roads to the hospital where my father might be dying.

I ignored the stinging pain in my palms and pushed my wheels again. Sweat rolled into my eyes, and my shoulders ached, but I had to get to him. Had to tell him I was sorry, and that I loved him, because if I didn't get the chance again, I'd never forgive myself.

Dirt billowed around me like a cloud and the first car I'd seen in an hour ignored my stuck-up thumb. I normally loved country living but right now I despised it. I hated that I'd had no phone reception when my mother had been leaving frantic voicemail messages on my phone, trying to tell me that my father had collapsed in the middle of one of our riding rings. I hated that I hadn't seen or heard the ambulance from the back end of the property in time to get to them before they'd gone tearing down the main road with my father on a stretcher and my mother by his side. I hated that there was no bus, or Uber, and that my wheelchair was not made for navigating these potholed roads.

My mouth was bone dry, and I was desperate for water when the rumble of a car engine sounded in the distance. Oh lord, please. A car. Any car. I lifted my head and brought one hand up to shield my eyes from the slowly sinking sun.

My stomach dropped.

Any car but that one.

I put my head down, stubbornly refusing to stick my thumb out and reasoning that it was probably only another ten kilometres, though the thought made me want to weep. Mr Ryker's rusted ute slowed anyway, and I gritted my teeth to keep my focus on the road. I didn't want to deal with him. There was nothing but bad blood between our family and the Rykers, and the old man was probably drunk. He always was by this time of the day. I needed to get to the hospital, not die in a car crash along the way.

The window rattled as it wound down. "Gemma."

I froze.

I hadn't heard that voice in four years, but there was no mistaking it. I whipped my head up, and sure enough, my gaze collided with Adam Ryker's chocolate-brown eyes. He sat behind the wheel of his father's car, with a baseball cap shoved low on his brow. He was a little older, a little more filled out than the teenager who'd once made my life a living hell, but still him all the same.

For a long moment, neither of us spoke, while my heart thumped unevenly. Then I turned away and shoved my wheels so hard they sent dirt flying. What was he doing back? He'd been gone for years. To where, I didn't know and I didn't care. I'd just liked knowing he wasn't going to ambush me on the side of the road. He was entitled to visit his father, but that didn't mean I had to have anything to do with him. He could visit, then go back to wherever it was he'd come from. Go back to blissfully being out of my life.

Boots thumped when they hit the dusty road, and a car door slammed. I pushed my chair harder, the sting of my open blisters only spurring me on faster. I choked back the sob rising in my throat. Damn him. This day was already a nightmare—him being here was just adding salt to the wound. His footsteps increased to a jog, and then he was in front of me, and I had no choice but to stop or run him over. Though the idea of mowing him down did give me a sick sense of pleasure.

"Gemma," he said again.

I suddenly hated my name.

"Stop."

"Leave me alone, Ryker. I've got somewhere I need to be."

"I can see that. Let me drive you."

I shook my head and tried to go around him, but he stepped in front of me.

I glared up at him. "Get out of my way."

"You're going to the hospital, right? I heard in town that your dad had been taken in an ambulance."

Of course he had. The gossip grapevine around small towns moved surprisingly fast considering how far apart people lived.

"Your hand is bleeding."

"No shit, Sherlock," I mumbled rudely.

He ignored me. "Please, Gemma, just get in. You must have been out here for hours to get this far. And I owe you one."

I snorted. He owed me a hell of a lot more than one. With every ounce of my being, I hated that he thought I needed his help. I didn't. I'd already made it more than halfway on my own. Admittedly, I was the worse for wear, but I knew I could make it the rest of the way.

But Ryker didn't appear to be moving, and I *was* desperate to see my father. Time alone on the side of the road gave me entirely too much time to think, and all I could think about was what a shit daughter I was.

"Fine," I gritted out, turning around and moving to the passenger side of the ute.

"Here, let me—"

He froze at the look I shot him then slowly he withdrew his hand. I opened the passenger door, grateful the ute was low to the ground, which always made transferring that bit easier. Then I hoisted myself into the seat, leant out to take the wheels off my chair, and collapsed the seat. Pulling the pieces into the dual cab, I placed them on the floor behind me.

Ryker hovered around my door looking unsure, until I slammed it in his face. That, I guess, gave him the hint that I didn't need his help. The tiniest of smiles lifted the corner of his mouth as he slid into the driver's seat. I pointedly ignored it while he put the gearstick in first and completed a U-turn on the wide road. To his credit, he didn't try to make any further conversation with me, and I stared out the passenger-side window with unseeing eyes, all too aware of how close he was. I just wanted to get to the hospital. Both to see my dad and to get the hell away from him.

Even facing away from him, he was everywhere. His scent drifted around the cab, fresh and clean compared to my dirt and sweat. And I'd swear I could feel him looking at me. The heat of his gaze on my back warmed my already too hot skin, and I wished he'd stop. I didn't need the little trip down memory lane his presence brought on. I didn't have it in me to do that right now.

The roads became paved as we travelled closer to town, and after we'd passed the two pubs and a handful of local shops on Main Street, Ryker pulled into our tiny country hospital. He stopped right at the door, though this time, he didn't try to help me. I reassembled my chair and shifted into it, banging my elbow in my haste to get out.

"Thank you," I said stiffly before I slammed the door and rolled to the entrance. I'd managed to make it through the whole car trip without looking directly at him. I was oddly proud of myself.

"You're welcome," he said quietly through the open window as the automatic doors whooshed open and admitted me into the cool interior of the hospital. They closed behind me, and a sigh of relief escaped me. With a bit of luck, it would be another four years before I had to see Adam Ryker again. Even better if I never did.

Keep reading here!

*Dangerous Little Secrets (Saint View High, #2)

*Twisted Little Truths (Saint View High, #3)

Saint View Prison - (Reverse Harem, Romantic Suspense)

Book 1: Locked Up Liars (Saint View Prison, #1)

Book 2: Solitary Sinners (Saint View Prison, #2)

Book 3: Fatal Felons (Saint View Prison, #3)

Add your email address here to be the first to know when new books are available!

www.ellethorpe.com/newsletter

Join Elle Thorpe's readers group on Facebook!

www.facebook.com/groups/ellethorpesdramallamas

ACKNOWLEDGMENTS

Firstly, I want to thank my Drama Llamas readers group. You guys are the best thing about Facebook! I love having a bunch of awesome women to hang out with and talk all things books and romance. If you aren't already in there, come find us! An extra big thank you to Debra Phiri for naming Damien for me.

To my promo team. I wish I had room to thank you all individually. Your reviews and reposts and photos and cheerleading are so important and so valued. Thank you.

To my editor, Emmy, from www.studioenp.com Thank you for all your hard work and for always being a complete pro.

To my amazing critique partners, Jolie Vines and Zoe Ashwood. Thanks for all the 5am sprints, the late night (or all night) chats, the advice, the feedback, the encouragement. I'd be lost without you both. Love you. Team Rabbit forever!

To my beta readers Shellie Maddison, Ally Murphy, Alisa Cavanaugh, Tamara McCall and Shannan Percival. Thank you all for loving this book and for not making me do too many edits! haha. You're such an important part of my process and I couldn't do it without you!

To Jira, Thomas, Felicity and Heidi. Thank you for always being my favourite people, even when you're driving me nuts. I love you.

And last but never least, thank you to you guys. The readers. Thank you for loving my characters the way I do.

Elle Thorpe lives on the sunny east coast of Australia. When she's not writing stories full of kissing, she's a wife and mummy to three tiny humans. She's also official ball thrower to one slobbery dog named Rollo. Yes, she named a female dog after a dirty hot character on Vikings. Don't judge her. Elle is a complete and utter fangirl at heart, obsessing over The Walking Dead and Outlander to an unhealthy degree. But she wouldn't change a thing.

You can find her on Facebook and Instagram (@ellethorpe-books or hit the links below!) or at her website www.ellethorpe.com

facebook.com/ellethorpebooks
instagram.com/ellethorpebooks
goodreads.com/ellethorpe
pinterest.com/ellethorpebooks